Giving Something Back

Best Regards

Robert Nicholas Hussey

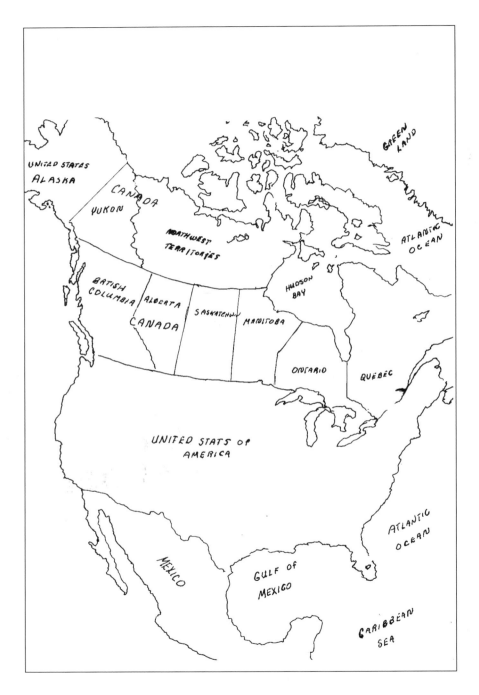

Giving Something Back

Robert Nicholas Kucey

Illustrations by Chris Bebonang

hancock
house

ISBN 0-88839-566-3
Copyright © 2004 Robert Nicholas Kucey

Cataloging in Publication Data

Kucey, Robert N., 1940–
    Giving something back / Robert Nicholas Kucey ;
    illustrations by Chris Bebonang.

    ISBN 0-88839-566-3

    I. Title.
PS8571.U247G48 2004   C813'.6   C2003-911214-4

Illustrations by Chris Bebonang

We acknowledge the financial support of the Government of Canada through the
Book Publishing Industry Development Program (BPIDP) for our publishing activities.

Published simultaneously in Canada and the United States by

HANCOCK HOUSE PUBLISHERS LTD.
19313 Zero Avenue, Surrey, B.C. V3S 9R9
(604) 538-1114 Fax (604) 538-2262

HANCOCK HOUSE PUBLISHERS
1431 Harrison Avenue, Blaine, WA 98230-5005
(604) 538-1114 Fax (604) 538-2262
Web Site:www.hancockhouse.com email:sales@hancockhouse.com

The Cutting Edge

With the completion of the recent revival meetings I have been sensing in my spirit a challenge from the Lord to remind us what revival really is. The Bible tells us that after the word of the Lord comes, "Satan comes immediately and takes away the word that was sown in their hearts" (Mark 4:15). He's out to destroy what has been given. Paul tells us in 2 Corinthians 2:11 that Satan can take advantage of us or outwit us if we are unaware of his schemes, so we need to stay alert and guard what God has done in our hearts. Keeping this in mind, I would like to encourage you with a few words today.

The key to revival is not found in formulas or steps; it's found in our desperate crying out to God for His manifested presence that will transform our lives. Revival is not about building churches, ministries, or having nightly services. It is not about healings, deliverance, or signs and wonders. These are all marks or byproducts of revival. Revival is you and I looking like Jesus. It is when the character of Christ emerges in our life, causing us to turn from evil and graciously endure trials. It is when our hearts are moved with compassion and mercy and we choose to intercede rather than be angry and judgmental. It is when we choose to love, forgive, and pray for those who persecute and offend us. It is when we choose to take the low ground of humility, recognizing our daily need of a Savior and Redeemer as we grow in holiness. Then we will depend on His strength rather than our own, realizing that it is His grace and not our works that enables us to walk in the truth of His word.

As we continue on our way in the days ahead, let's remember not to be discouraged by what we see or hear. Rather, let's be encouraged as we walk in obedience to Jesus, allowing His love to change us, then flow through us to others.

Blessings,

Laura Masson

Contents

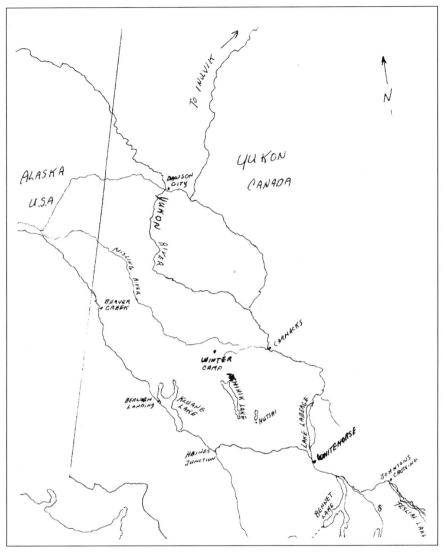

Winter Camp in the Yukon

CHAPTER 1

Going Up to the Yukon

NICK ROBERTS took a year off his busy Vancouver real estate practice and went up to the Yukon. He needed to escape a tension-filled job, the constant stress of city life, and a two-year relationship that had faded away. Leaving behind painful memories, he was bound and determined to spend the rest of his days by himself. Nevertheless, at fifty-one years of age there was emptiness in his life, he longed for family and the laughter of children.

While in the Yukon, he stayed on his friends buffalo ranch. Cliff and Virginia owned a three-thousand-acre ranch, about thirty miles west of Whitehorse on the Alaska Highway. It lay tucked away in the splendor of a lush green valley, surrounded by the majesty of snow-capped mountains. The large log ranch house, with its second-storey balcony, overlooked a broad expanse of green fields that swept across a fertile basin. Inside the comfortable rambling home, an inviting kitchen held an old-fashioned wood-burning cook stove with two huge ovens and enough cooking area to prepare meals for at least forty people.

A short distance from the main house stood a large garage and two smaller buildings. One housed the lone hired hand, the other, a two-bedroom trailer overlooking a small horse corral, was where Nick stayed. His trailer, near the entrance to the ranch, was surrounded by a thick grove of spruce trees that opened onto a small pond where several white geese wallowed away each and every afternoon in the cool pristine waters.

Nick liked spending time with Cliff and Virginia. A little over sixty-five years of age, Cliff looked as though he'd had a tough life, yet he always had a ready smile and a way of making even a total stranger feel at ease. Virginia, perhaps twenty years younger than her husband, was an attractive woman who kept herself in great physical shape. Most days she could be found cutting wood with

The Buffalo Ranch

a chainsaw, hauling truckloads of water for her flourishing garden, or doing any number of chores around the ranch.

In the Yukon the land, trees and air, all seemed to be much cleaner and fresher than anywhere else. Even the white snow-capped mountains, looked a little brighter than any he had ever seen. In his bones he could feel the beauty of this land, and what it had to offer. Although it was his first time in the Yukon, it felt familiar, as though he had traveled this land before.

As a boy, Nick Roberts had grown up in the wilderness, living on the Dauphin River Indian Reservation. His father operated a fish shed and general store, buying fish from the Indians and selling groceries, clothing, nets, and other supplies. Being non-native and living on a reservation, Nick soon learned many of their ancient ways. He was taught how to survive in the wilderness, and to live in it with harmony. He also knew that whenever the Indians took something from nature, they give something back, maintaining a balance between themselves and the land they occupied.

Nick's memories of the Indians were a warm, caring, compassionate people, very knowledgeable about their environment. They could forecast the weather by the type of clouds in the sky and the direction in which they moved. They were also very good hunters, trappers, and fisherman. When they read a set of tracks, they would know what kind of animal made them, how big it was, and how fast it had been traveling. They walked through the bush so silently that the animals would not hear them and they always looked back to see if anything had crossed behind. They could track an animal for days without getting lost, using mostly the sun in the daytime and the stars at night to find their direction. They also knew that moss grew on the north side of dead trees and stumps. From these observations, they could figure out which way was east, west, or south. A young Nick Roberts spent time in the woods with the Indians every opportunity he had and over the years he learned a great deal about their ancient ways.

In his youth he had loved the wilderness, and now visiting with Cliff and Virginia on their Yukon ranch brought back many fond memories of his childhood.

After a week of visiting Nick grew restless. He took a job driving a supply trucks from Whitehorse to Beaver Creek on the Yukon-Alaska border. Averaging three trips a week, each one lasted from fourteen to eighteen hours, and he enjoyed it thoroughly. In his spare time he helped Cliff with odd jobs around the ranch, and sometime fished the nearby lakes or streams.

While driving the supply truck, Nick met a number of very interesting people. Maybe because of its remoteness, most were very friendly and open. Driving back and forth, he befriended some of the people who flagged for various construction companies. One young lady in particular, who flagged for the Yukon Highways Department, stood out above the rest. During their first conversation he learned her name was Miranda, she was three-quarters Tutchone, and lived near the village of Carmacks. On the next trip through, she told him she was a single mother with two children and was working with the contraction crew for the summer. "I need to earn a little extra income to help pay for my correspondence courses," she told him.

"What are you studying," Nick asked.

"Wildlife biology," she said but their conversation ended when the vehicles in his line began to move.

On one of their brief road encounters, after Nick told her he loved fishing and hunting, he found it quite amusing when she said: "Even though I'm an Indian I've never learned how to gut a moose."

Joking, he replied: "Don't worry Miranda, maybe someday I'll teach you how."

Over the next three or four months, their conversation would go something like, "Hi Miranda. Having a good day?"

Miranda always had a smile on her face when Nick pulled up with the truck. "No! It's too dusty out here. Not enough wind to blow it away, but other then that, okay I guess. By the way, when are you going to teach me how to gut a moose?"

"Gut a moose?" he paused and then smiled as he remembered. "We have to shoot one first Miranda. This fall I'm planning on hunting moose not far from your home of Carmacks. Maybe you'd like to come along, for a day or two."

"That doesn't sounds to bad. Don't forget to... Sorry, here comes the pilot car. Talk to you later," she said, moving down the road.

Each time Nick bumped into her after that, there wasn't any mention of hunting, then by early September the roadwork ended and she was gone.

Before going south for the winter, Nick headed to the Nisling Valley to hunt moose. The Nisling Valley was where several years earlier, the Canadian government had built a steel buffalo corral, surrounded by eight miles of wire fencing. It was part of a program to reintroduce the wood buffalo back into the Yukon, after more than a hundred year absence.

Following the release of ten herds of about thirty animals each into different parts of the valley, the government was satisfied that the population was strong enough to sustain itself and they disbanded the project.

Early that spring, Nick went in as part if Cliff's crew to remove the corral and wire fencing. While in the valley, he spotted a large number of moose and knew it would be a good place to hunt in the fall. He had bought an old tepee from Jerry Beaumont, a Métis Indian; he worked with on the crew. It was in excellent condition and at a very reasonable price. Nick couldn't pass up a bargain.

An imposing figure, Jerry stood out from the rest of the crew not just because of his six-foot-four-inch frame and the distinctive huge moustache, but also a large cowboy hat added even more to his immensity. Adorned with an eagle feather, through work, meals, conversation, and even when he slept, the hat never left the man's head. No matter what he did, or where he went, somehow the huge feather survived it all in tact. Tilted forward slightly over

Inside the tepee.

his eyes when he lay on his back sleeping, Jerry's hat soon became a topic of whispered conversation amongst the work crew members as to who might have the courage to try and steal the feather in the middle of the night. No one did.

Nick instantly liked the man, and after the second day on the job they sat next to each other at lunch break, talking about their mutual interests: hunting and fishing. Nick soon learned that during the summer months Jerry worked at whatever manual labor jobs were available but only long enough and hard enough to do what he really enjoyed when winter came. Jerry had run a trap line every winter for as long as he could remember, something his father, and his father before him, had done.

During one of their conversations, Nick told Jerry of his intention to hunt moose here in the fall.

"You should, this is a great area for game," Jerry's long arm instinctively swept across the wilderness scene in front of them. "In fact, the end of my trap line isn't far from here."

Nick Roberts set up his tepee, beside a stream, located about a mile and a half from the end of an abandoned mining-camp road, not far from where the buffalo compound once stood.

Even though, planning on to stay for only a few weeks, he

made several trips on foot to his pickup truck, transporting necessities for living in the wilderness. Once he had the tepee assembled, he cut an adequate supply of firewood. After that, in anticipation of a successful moose hunt, he set about building a smokehouse, drying racks, and a high cache, all constructed the way the Indians had taught him many years ago.

Although there was no real need to be meticulous, for nearly a week he worked from dawn till dusk, making the place exactly the way he wanted. Rising early every day, eating hearty meals, and living in the clean fresh air amidst the vast tranquility of the Yukon, invigorated him, bringing a peace he had not felt in a long time.

When he finished the work on his campsite, he blazed a trail to the far side of the ridge where he built a lookout tower atop the tallest tree in the area. For hunting, this strategic vantage point would provide a clear view of both the valley on the one side and the large swampy area on the other.

With his camp all set up; Nick drove the sixty-five miles to the village of Carmacks to replenish his supplies. While shopping in the food store, he heard a soft voice behind him.

"Hi, stranger." Nick paid little attention, thinking it wasn't for him until the voice came again, this time a little louder. "Hi, Nick — Nick Roberts?"

Nick turned to see the smiling face of a young lady standing near one of the aisles. At her side were two children. It took a minute before he recognized the girl from the road construction crew. He had forgotten that Miranda had told him she lived in this area and on those previous occasions whenever they met, her face had been dusty, her hair tucked under a hard hat, and she had always worn a pair of baggy orange coveralls. But the woman standing in front of him seemed a different person entirely.

Immaculately dressed in a red sweater and white slacks, her clean face shone and her long black hair, adorned with a red ribbon, hung halfway down her back. Despite having only seen her in work clothes he had always thought her attractive. But now, with only a small amount of makeup, he found her strikingly beautiful.

For a moment Nick Roberts could only stare, then he managed to say: "Oh, hi, Miranda. Good to see you. How are you?"

"I'm fine," she said, moving closer as she spoke. "So you are here to do some hunting?"

"Yes," he replied, surprised she remembered. "I've just finished setting up a campsite where the old buffalo compound used to be. I just came into town for supplies." He looked at the children near her. "These must be the two you told me about."

"Yes, this is Leah, and the one over there is Joseph."

"Hi, Leah. Hi, Joseph," Nick greeted them.

The young girl, large brown eyes cast timidly downward, gave a faint hello, as the curious five-year-old clung a little tighter to her mother. The boy mumbled only a curt hello, then turned and walked away.

"Sorry Nick," Miranda said, giving a frustrated shrug of her shoulders and rolling her eyes.

"That's okay, we all have bad days." Then Nick smiled and asked, "How old is he?"

"He just turned seven."

"Mom, can we have some of those candies? —— You promised," Joseph hollered from the next aisle.

"Yes, but first, young man, you will come back here and apologize to Mr. Roberts for your rude behavior," Miranda fumed.

The boy appeared at the end of the aisle. "Hello," he said resignedly, still only glancing in Nick's direction.

After they had spoken for a few minutes, Miranda asked if he would like to come over to her place for tea before heading back to the woods. Nick looked at his watch and she quickly added: "Maybe I can I tempt you with fresh apple pie, too. I've got one cooling on the window ledge."

"In that case, lead the way!" he beamed, handing the clerk his money.

"Give me two minutes to finish here and you can follow me home," Miranda said.

Nick had to make several trips to load all his purchases in the truck. By the time he finished, Miranda was waiting beside her car.

At her home, Nick was drinking tea and finishing off a second piece of pie when Miranda asked, "Nick, were you serious when you promised to teach me how to gut a moose?"

"Sure, why, do you want to come along?"

"When does the season open?" She asked.

13

"Next Saturday morning."

"And how long do you intend to stay out there?"

"I had planned to stay two or three weeks, but you can come back any time you want."

"If I come, where would I sleep?"

"I set up a tepee, not far from where the old buffalo compound used to be. You can sleep there. I prefer to sleep outside in a hammock I have strung between two trees. If it rains, you won't stay out there anyway." Despite being a perpetual loner, somehow Nick felt a growing enthusiasm for the idea.

Miranda seemed pleased at his words. "I think I'd really enjoy it. Are you sure you wouldn't mind having me tag along?"

"Not at all, it would be nice having company for a change."

"I have my own sleeping bag and my late husband's rival. What else would you like me to bring?"

"Just some warm clothing in case it turns cold."

"What should I bring for food?"

"Maybe the rest of that apple pie," Nick joked then added. No, I have plenty."

"Okay, so where should I meet you?"

"You can drive up to the end of the old mining-camp road early Saturday morning and I'll be waiting for you. Can you be there by seven-thirty?"

"No problem. I'll see you then." She beamed with enthusiasm.

Nick said good-bye to Miranda and her children. Once again, her young daughter was all smiles while the boy only mumbled.

On his way to the village, Nick spotted an outfitter's sign on side of the road. Thinking he might have a horse to rent, Nick pulled into the driveway.

A tall, gangly, leathery-faced man, wearing a straw hat, answered the door. When Nick introduced himself and explained his need for a horse, the man laughed and said he had one — sort of. "It's been running loose in the valley all summer and I haven't had the inclination to go after it." The man paused, sizing Nick up. "Tell you what. That darn horse won't be too far from where you say you set up camp. You catch her, and you can use her for as long as you want."

Nick thanked the man and said he thought he would at least

look around for the horse. After borrowing some rope and a halter, just in case, Nick drove back to his camp.

Walking through the woods, his thoughts turned to hunting with Miranda and he wondered if she really would show up. Up to now, they were little more than two people who had met several times along a highway and talked. But, truth be known, he very much looked forward to sharing the time with someone with a wonderful personality that made him feel so at ease.

CHAPTER 2

Miranda

ALL SMILES, and immensely pleased with himself at having captured the horse, Saturday morning Nick Roberts arrived at the turnoff to meet Miranda. Not having a saddle or bridle, he rode bareback, using only a rope halter to control the horse.

Miranda showed up just before seven-thirty, pulled into a clearing at the side of the road and hurriedly stepped from her car.

"Good morning," her cheery voice greeted him. Wearing jeans, a heavy sweater, a baseball cap with a long braid of hair hanging down her back, and heavy boots, she was ready for a few days of roughing it. "Where on earth did you get the horse?" she asked, removing a large packsack and a rifle from the vehicle.

He explained the outfitter's offer, and the many hours spent capturing the horse. "A few apples, and a lot of patience," he laughed.

"I brought enough warm clothing to last a week, but I hope it won't take us that long to get a moose. I left the kids with their father's mom. Even though grandma loves them, at her age after three or four days she's usually had enough."

"There are fresh tracks along the ridge and yesterday I caught glimpse of a moose running along the river. With a little luck, we should have one in a day or two."

Nick mounted the horse and stretched out a rigid boot toe so that Miranda could step on it while he helped her climb on behind him.

She told him she had ridden a horse only once before and was a little nervous. Hanging tight to Nick's waist, they rode the mile and a half into camp. When they turned into the clearing where he had set up his tepee, Miranda was genuinely surprised at how Nick had everything so well set up.

"Wow, it looks like you've been living here all summer! I like the tepee, but what's that building over there?" she asked, pointing to a small structure on their right.

"That's the smokehouse for that big moose you're going to shoot!"

Nick lifted her down from the horse and carried her belongings into the tepee. "Miranda, we still have time to get in a good morning's hunt," he told her as she quickly organized her things. "I built a tree stand on the other side of the ridge that you can easily climb up to sit in, while I circle around through the swamp. If a moose comes out, you should be able to get a clear shot at it."

"Sounds good," she said, picking up her rifle and dropping a box of bullets in her jacket pocket. "I'm ready to go."

At the lookout, she climbed up to sit on the small platform, Nick followed and passing up her rifle. As he climbed back down the tree, with a sly smiled he said, "If you see something coming through the woods, make sure it's the moose you shot, not me. I'm the one without the antlers!"

Nick spent more than two hours making his way around the ridge and through the swamp back to Miranda's lookout. From her high perch, she spotted him coming half a mile away. She waved from high in the tree and by the time Nick got there, she had climbed down and was waiting for him.

"Well, did you see anything?" he wanted to know.

"Yes. I saw one without antlers — You!" she said, playfully punching him in the shoulder.

After lunch, Miranda helped Nick plug some of the cracks in the smokehouse. He built it using three-inch-thick willow poles bound together with strands of cedar root. The smokehouse, four feet by four feet wide and a little less than six feet high, had a roof that sloped to the back. Flat rocks covered the floor and large round stones bordered each side. Even if the fire went out, the smokehouse remained warm for a long time.

At three-thirty in the afternoon they tried the same hunt as in the morning, with the same negative results. It was dark by the time they got back to camp. As soon as they had eaten dinner and washed the dishes, they were both ready for a good night's sleep.

Nick was up before dawn and had tea ready by the time Miranda was awake and dressed. He wanted her in the stand no later than six-thirty. Still dark when they left the tepee, the fall air

Bull moose.

was crisp, clear, and cold, with a heavy frost on the ground that helped make it a perfect morning for tracking.

Nick circled to the east this time and stayed up in the high country. At about ten o'clock, he heard the echo of a shot coming from the direction of the tree stand. More than a half-mile away he hurried as fast as he could but by the time he arrived at the stand, he found it to be empty. Gravely concerned for her safety, he hollered as loud as he could, "MIRANDA!"

"Over here, — in the gully. I got one! Come quick!" she screamed.

Nick ran down to the ravine and saw Miranda standing over one of the biggest bull-moose he'd ever seen, with antlers the size of Christmas trees. Miranda was bursting with excitement but then gave Nick a puzzled look and asked, "Now what do I do?"

"What you wanted to do all summer. Gut it!" he answered with a bit of a chuckle.

He pointed out a few old Indian tricks and helping out a bit. After she'd finished, he gave her a hand skinning, and cutting it up. Nick went back to camp and got the horse and a roll of cheesecloth for wrapping the meat. He returned on horseback to where Miranda was waiting and together they loaded the moose meat and brought it back to camp. Exhausted, they washed up in the stream then took a short break, lighting a fire and making fresh tea.

Nick hung pieces of meat in the smokehouse while Miranda cut some of it into strips and placed them on the drying racks. The remainder, they stored in the hole Nick had dug into the permafrost where the meat would freeze. The storage hole, four feet deep and three feet square, was lined with cedar boughs and covered with heavy logs to protect it from animals. A small shelf near

Miranda gutting the moose.

19

the top, made from sticks bound together, kept other things cool without freezing. This far north, a simple hole in the ground was as good as a refrigerator.

By the time they finished putting all the meat away it was nine o'clock and darkness had set in. Dead tired, they ate a quick supper and said goodnight.

In the morning, after breakfast, Miranda gathered together her things and Nick packed up a few choice pieces of moose meat for her to take home.

At her car, she placed her things in the trunk then hesitated after opening the driver's door. For a moment she seemed about to say something but instead, she slid into the seat, adjusting her body behind the wheel. She rolled the window down and looking at Nick, paused again. Finally she spoke: "Nick, would it be alright if I brought my kids out here next Saturday to show them your camp and everything you've built?"

"Of course," he told her. "They cane come for the weekend, if you want."

"Really, are you sure? Joseph is well, you know — difficult at times. You've seen how he can be."

"Don't give it a second thought. A weekend for him with nature might be just what the doctor ordered."

Relieved, and visibly happy, Miranda thanked him again. After agreeing to meet at the same place at four-thirty the following Friday afternoon, they said good-bye. Nick sat on his horse, watching until her car disappeared in the distance.

Up at the crack of dawn, Nick bathed in the cold stream. Shivering, he rushed to the tepee to dry off. After a good breakfast, he lit a fire in the smokehouse and began the lengthy process of tanning the moose hide. The first few hours were spent carefully scraping away all the bits of flesh and fat from the large hide. When there was not a speck of flesh left he turned the hide over and applied a paste to the hairy side. The paste, made from the ash of burnt oak wood, would take three or four days to have it full effect. When it did, the hair would be loose enough to be easily pulled out. Then with the hair removed, he would make a pole frame that the hide could be tightly laced to. Stretched and secured taut to the frame, a fire under the hide would allow the smoke to slowly cure the leather. The whole tanning process would take over two weeks from start to finish.

Alone in the woods, without a worry in the world, Nick Roberts had time to do as he pleased. With the river full of fat salmon making their way upstream to spawn, early one morning he dug out a jar of salted salmon roe from his tackle box, picked up his fishing rod, and wandered down to the river. The water was low as it hadn't rained for over a month and immediately he spotted several large, bright red-and-green salmon in the shallows along the shore. He attached a ball of salmon roe to his line and threw it into the current, letting it slowly drift downstream. It wasn't long before he'd caught two good-sized king salmon; one he guessed weighed about twenty-five pounds and the other almost forty pounds.

He hung up most of his catch in the smokehouse, the rest he sliced into thin strips and spread them on the drying racks in the sun. There was more fish than one person could eat in a month. For the bald eagle that had been hanging around camp for the past week, he spread the bones and intestines on the rocks.

Keeping busy made the days go by quickly. The next thing he knew, it was Friday afternoon, time to get the horse ready and meet Miranda and her children at the cut-off. He arrived there at a quarter past four, just as she was pulling in. As soon as Joseph and Leah hopped out of the car, they ran straight to the horse.

Drying racks.

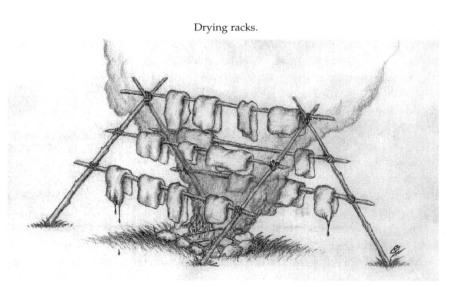

"Can we pet him Mr. Nick? Will he bite?" An excited Leah wanted to know.

"It's a she, Leah, you can pet her. And no, she won't bite." Nick told her. Then she asked what his name was.

"J H! Nick said.

"JH! That's a funny name for a horse." Miranda and the children spoke the same words in unison.

"Well," Nick paused, "I didn't really know her name, so JH stands for, Just Horse."

The children stared at him and Miranda burst into laughter.

A slightly embarrassed Nick needed to change the subject and quickly said: "If your mother says its okay, the two of you can ride the horse to camp."

A still grinning Miranda nodded her approval.

After loading and tying their supplies to the travois, Nick lifted Leah onto the horse's back. A defiant Joseph said he didn't need any help; he could get on by himself. After three or four tries, he begrudgingly let Nick help him up.

The travois was made using two poles in parallel, one on either side of the horse. It was bound together by pieces of leather. A strap over the horse's neck and around its chest secured the travois in place. The back section, held apart by two small wooden slats, had a canvas laced into the center. Indians used them for hauling everything, including people.

Leading the horse by the halter, Nick and Miranda slowly walked side by side to the campsite. Holding tight onto the travois poles, on the horse's bare back the children swayed gently to and fro, talking and laughing all the way.

As soon as they emerged from the trail into the clearing where Nick's tepee stood, excited children jumped from the horse's back and raced around, checking out everything.

"Can I go fishing?" Joseph said, emerging from the tepee with Nick's fishing rod in his hand.

Before Nick could speak, Miranda ran to her son. "Joseph, put that back. You know better than to take someone's property without asking."

The boy gave his mother a disgusted look then turned on his heel and entered the tent.

Nick treated them to some of his fresh bannock while it was

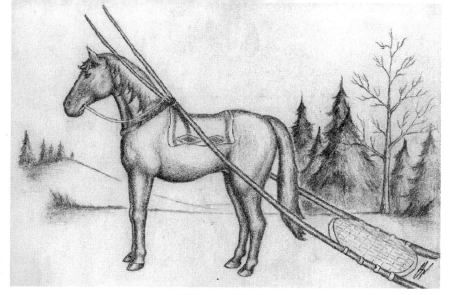

Horse and travois.

still warm. He bathed it in butter and honey and two hungry children quickly devoured their pieces. Leah wanted to know what bannock was and Nick explained: "Bannock is something like bread the Indians made. They used flour, water, baking powder, and a little salt mixed together, flattened out and baked in a skillet over an open fire."

"Yummy," Joseph showed the first smile, since Nick had met him. "Can I have more?"

"Me too," Leah piped up.

"You sure know how to make a chef feel good!" Nick laughed, reaching to affectionately rub the children on the head. "Maybe we should leave a little room for supper. But before bed, we could sneak another piece. How does that sound, guys?"

"Great!" came a unified reply.

The children wanted to see the beehive where Nick had gotten the fresh honey. It wasn't far, so in the growing dusk he walked with them through the woods and up a small hill to where he had found the large beehive. Nick lit a dry chunk of tree bark, showing the children how he used smoke to calm the bees while gathering honey, without getting stung. To get to the honey, Nick carefully opened the side of the hive he had cut into earlier, and showed the children the honeycomb inside.

"Hey! There's still some honey left. Why don't we take it?" Joseph said when peering into the hive.

Nick explained that it was important to leave enough honey in the bee's hive to ensure they had food to survive the long winter.

Miranda looked up from where she was kneeling by the fire as the trio emerged from woods into the campsite clearing. "Mom," an excited Joseph ran to her. "You should see where honey comes from. It's amazing!"

"Chicken!" Nick said, leaning over to look at the pieces sizzling in the cast-iron frying pan. "Looks good — real good."

"I thought you might be tired of moose meat so…"

"You're right, chicken is a real treat," Nick broke in. "Thanks." He moved to sit on the large flat stone near the fire.

The hearty meal included potatoes, turnips, and carrots boiled with onions, heaped on metal platters. The children ate most of their food; the issue of more bannock now forgotten.

Finished eating, Nick rose from his place and turned to look at Joseph. "Your mom worked hard to make us a good meal. How about if you and I show her our appreciation and we go wash the dishes in the stream?"

"Sure," Joseph leapt to his feet. Miranda shook her head in amazement.

With the dishes done and things tidied up, they gathered around the fire. Joseph appointed himself in charge of keeping the fire going, every few minutes adding another small log until he grew tired and curled up next to his mother.

Before long he started dozing off, Nick carried him into the tepee and Miranda tucked him into bed. Leah, still wide awake wanted to stay up. The three of them remained around the campfire talking for some time, before they all finally decided to turn in for the night.

Early in the morning, while the others were still asleep, Nick slipped from his hammock, lit the cooking fire and added logs to the one still simmering in the smokehouse. He turned the salmon on the drying racks then, in the invigorating morning sunshine, sauntered down to the stream to get a pail of water. By the time he wandered back to the campsite, Miranda and the children were up preparing breakfast.

"You're spoiling me," he teased, placing the water pail on the small wood table and sniffing at the pan of sizzling bacon. "I'm not used to having someone wait on me. — Anything I can do?"

"No thanks. The children are doing just fine. Get yourself a plate; it'll be ready in a few minutes."

After a breakfast they walked down to the stream to watch the salmon make their run, in the shallow waters. Downstream, splashing sounds drew their attention to three large brown bears. To get a better look, and to give the animals some space, Nick picked the children up in his arms and climbed the small slope to the crest of a hill. In the sunny fall morning with all the leaves off the trees, they had a clear view through the bush.

For a while they watched the bears catch fish, later they hiked through the woods along the edge of the stream to where the old buffalo compound once stood. Nick told Miranda about his working here earlier in the year, after he arrived in the Yukon. He also told her how he met Jerry, the Métis, who sold him the tepee.

On the return walk, Nick spotted a tall clump of weeds growing at the edge of a pond. Using his knife, he cup down some of the swamp grass and carried a large bundle of it back to camp. That night, sitting around the fire, Nick showed the children how the Indians made simple woven baskets, from the flat wide swamp grass. Leah was eager to learn, but Joseph stayed quiet. His good mood was gone and he had no interest in participating. Nick didn't know why, but the boy certainly had a chip on his shoulder and Miranda said that his behavior was often distant and sullen. In future, Nick thought, he would try to discreetly direct most of his attention to Joseph without hurting little Leah's feelings.

After the children were in bed, he and Miranda were relaxing around the fire; Nick told her that he had decided to spend the winter, here in the bush. He said it was something he had always wanted to do and he felt he was up to the challenge. "I'm not ready to go back to the hectic pace of business just yet. More time in this place is awfully appealing," he looked at her as though seeking her approval.

Miranda thought that despite his wilderness skills, it was a pretty daring thing to do all by himself. She knew that once Nick had made up his mind to do something, his character was so strong that he would do it.

On Sunday, they woke to dark skies and in the middle of

breakfast a light rain started to fall. Clutching their plates of food, they all rushed back inside the tepee. With the pelting rain making outdoor activities impossible, Nick offered to tell the children a story. Both children nodded their heads and Leah moved to sit down next to him.

"Well, let's see. Remember when you guys asked me why I used smoke in the beehive? I told you I would tell you the story when we had more time. Well now we got the time." Nick said, rubbing the stubble on his chin.

"I was about Joseph's age, when one of the Indians on the reservation told me the story about a young Indian boy named Okata. It seems Okata liked to sit in the meadows for hours watching the bees gathering honey from the flowers. One day he asked the bees if they would share some of their honey with him and his family. *No*, the bees scowled, *we've worked too hard gathering up all the honey. We're not sharing it with anyone!* When Okata tried to take a little of the honey from the hive, the bees stung him. He ran home and showed his father his arm, which by then was badly swollen from the bee stings. Okata's father was upset and led Okata to the high place near the village where he told the Great Spirit what had happened. The Great Spirit was not pleased with the bad behavior of the bees and soon made a huge forest fire, destroying all the beehives. The following winter the bees were very hungry and cold; many of them died. When the bees asked the Great Spirit why she had made the huge forest fire that had destroyed all their hives, she told them it was because they were too greedy and had refused to share some of their honey with Okata and his family. Since then, whenever a little smoke enters the hive, it reminds the bees of the day the Great Spirit made the huge forest fire — and that's the end of my story."

"I liked your story, Nick," Joseph said, a pleased look on his face.

"The rain has stopped," Miranda spoke, moving towards the tepee entrance and peering out. "I think maybe we should pack up and leave before the rain starts again."

CHAPTER 3

Jerry

THE CONSTANT CRACK of an axe resonated across the valley, as Nick Roberts, his shirt drenched with perspiration, drove himself to cut wood for the long cold winter ahead. But, one sweat-filled afternoon, he decided to cheat a little.

Smiling to himself and thinking that here in the woods he had no clock to punch, no deadline to meet, nor any of the other demands of his job in Vancouver. He put away his axe and with fishing rod in hand, wandered down to the stream.

Tossing a line in the water, he watched it drift lazily downstream. With a sigh of relief, he sat back against an old log, basking in the late morning sun. He had no idea how much time had passed when behind him, he heard a faint sound. Rising slightly and turning, his eyes scoured the bush for any sign of movement. In the distance, along the crest of the ridge, something was moving. Sharp eyes focused on the figure of a man on horseback, making his way down the hill. Whoever he was, the man rode tall in the saddle, moving in unison as though he and the horse were one. As horse and rider drew closer, the unmistakable sight of the long feather protruding from the rider's hat, told him exactly who it was.

"Over here," Nick called out, waving an arm.

The rider hesitated, looked in his direction and waved back, then detoured through a dense stand of alder, soon emerging in the glade by the stream. Dismounting from his big appaloosa stallion, a smiling Jerry Beaumont reached out to shake hands.

"Man, what a surprise! It's sure good to see you again." Nick said as he stepped forward to grasp Jerry's hand. "How did you find me? Are you out trapping already?"

"No, I'm just setting up the boxes for the traps. The season doesn't open for another few weeks."

Jerry on his Appaloosa stallion.

"You can spend a couple of days with me, I hope." Nick asked.

"Unfortunately, I have a load of wood to deliver so I'll have to leave sometime tomorrow."

"Come on over to the camp and see how I've set up your old tepee," Nick said, picking up his fishing rod and reeling in the line.

"Hop on behind," Jerry said.

"No need, the tepee is just a few yards through the bushes," Nick said, moving to walk alongside Jerry's horse.

A moment later they stepped into the clearing and crossed over to the campsite. Pausing at the fire, Nick poked the coals, and placed a dry log on top. While Jerry unsaddled his horse, Nick brewed a pot of fresh tea.

"Hey, Nick? Where did you get the horse?" Jerry called from inside the corral.

"From a local outfitter — but I had to catch it first."

"You had to catch it?"

"A long story," Nick replied. "I'll tell you about it later."

"So, city boy, you know how to ride, do you?"

"I seem to be able to stay on."

"Sure, maybe when that old nag's sleepin'," Jerry needled him.

"Don't laugh man. For all you know, she might just be the fastest thing on four legs north of the 60th parallel."

"Yeah, if you loaded her on a freight train first — Got a little hay for a real horse?"

"What, and waste my good hay on that beast of yours!" Nick shot back. "Aw, go ahead, we can't let it starve."

Over tea, the easy banter continued until a serious Jerry said how impressed he was with what Nick had managed to do in such a short time. "It looks like you've pretty well taken over this part of the woods!" he looked around. "How long are you planning on staying out here, anyway?"

"All winter."

"You've gotta be kiddin'!"

"Nope, dead serious."

"My friend, the winters here are a longer and a heck of a lot colder than in the big city, ya know. Are you plannin' on stayin' all winter in the tepee, or are you gonna build yourself a cabin?"

"I'm going to stay in the tepee." Nick said. Standing up, he added: "Come on, I'll show you what I've done with your tepee."

Taking his mug of tea and walking around to the back of the tepee, Jerry examined it closely.

"I banked the sides with moss and dried leaves to keep it warm." Nick pointed at his handiwork.

Jerry looked the tepee up and down, scratching and shaking his head as he did. Finally, he spoke. "I can't understand why on earth you wanna spend the winter in that thing, when you have a nice comfortable apartment in the city?"

"Jerry, do you have any idea how crowded the cities are getting? It seems that no matter where you go, you're always in a rush yet somehow always in a line up. I need a little time just to get away from it all and out here I feel relaxed and alive."

Jerry shook his head. "Well, I guess if you've made up your mind to spend the winter out here," he said, lightly tapping on the tepee's canvas. "The first thing you have to do is get rid of all those leaves. The moss is fine, but you gotta cover them with cedar boughs. It keeps the snow and ice from pushing in the sides," Jerry waved his long arms. "The cedar will also keep the moss underneath dry, and help keep in the heat."

"I haven't seen any cedar in this area," Nick said.

"There's some not too far north of here. I'll show you where on my way out tomorrow."

"Hungry?" Nick asked.

"Like a bear," Jerry grinned.

After lunch, Jerry offered to help Nick cut wooden poles to enlarge the tiny corral. With the two of them working, the job was nearly finished before the early fall darkness set in. Pleased with their effort, the two men put the tools in the tepee then relaxed around the large bonfire sipping mugs of hot tea.

Jerry told Nick that his trapping routine meant he would be checking this end of his line about every three weeks so if time permitted, he might drop by again. They ate a hearty supper and afterwards talked for some time until Jerry glanced at his watch. "Wow, its half past nine already. Maybe we better turn in."

"I could sit here and talk all night, but I guess we had better get a little sleep." Turning sideways, he pointed towards the hammock in the trees to the right of the tepee. "I prefer sleeping out here, Jerry. But, you can grab one of the beds inside the tepee and I'll see you in the morning."

"Out here is fine for me, too." Jerry untied his bedroll from the back of his saddle and spread it on the ground by the fire. "Have a good night, see you in the morning."

By dawn, a dense fog had rolled in blanketing the valley floor. Above the mist, along the jagged mountain ridge, a bright sun played hide and seek amongst the clouds. In the cool air, filled with the aroma of fresh coffee percolating, the two friends donned their heavy coats as they prepared breakfast over an open fire.

Nick placed two frying pans on the grate. One he filled with thick slices of bacon, the other he brushed with moose fat and dropped in six eggs. While he did, Jerry toasted bannock over hot coals, smothering them with butter before setting them on a rack beside the fire to keep warm. For these two friends, life couldn't get much better. They ate breakfast with little conversation, when finished, washed the dishes in the stream and headed for the corral.

Tossing the saddle over his horse's back, Jerry couldn't resist baiting Nick one more time.

"Hope you can keep up. I'd like to be home before dark."

Nick put the rope halter over the mare's head. "How far is that clump of cedar?"

"About two miles." Jerry answered, looking over at Nick. In a mocking voice he added: "Why, do you wanna race?"

Nick grabbed onto the horses mane and in one motion, swung his leg over and sat bareback on the mare, looking down at his friend. "All right, your on. — Go!"

"Son-of-a-gun," Jerry scrambled to finish saddling the horse as Nick darted out of the corral and across the clearing. After fastening his bedroll across the back of the saddle, he stepped into the stirrups and mounted the big stallion. At a tug of the bit, the horse danced sideways, turned around and bolted through the corral gate in hot pursuit of Nick and the mare.

Jerry dug in his heels and with a loud "yahoo," urged the horse forward. Within seconds, the appaloosa was flying through the bush trail without any sign of Nick. Reaching the open prairie, Jerry saw the dust cloud several hundred yards ahead. Mumbling to himself that maybe that old nag was a little spryer than he figured, he let the horse have full rein.

The powerful stallion ate up ground at a blistering pace and within minutes the two horses were neck and neck. But Nick had more horse than Jerry figured and urging his horse on, the valiant mare edged slightly ahead. For three-quarters of a mile, hooves thundered amidst billowing clouds of dust as they stormed across the dry ground of the open prairie.

As they approached the woodland, Jerry turned to look at Nick. With a wicked grin, he shouted: "Eat dust, my friend" and the stallion, its powerful legs digging deep into the hard clay surged forward leaving Nick in his wake.

Choking on the thick dust, Nick pushed the mare harder when all of a sudden a large feather went floating by. Glancing back, he almost collided with a hatless Jerry, racing back in the opposite direction. Laughing, Nick seized the opportunity and charged through the path in the woods. A quarter of the way up the side of the hill, Jerry caught up with him and when the path widened a little, he blew on by.

At the fork in the trail, Jerry glanced back and motioned with his arm for Nick to follow left. But for a resolute Nick, missing the signal and bolted straight through, it was too late. All at once the sight of a steep drop down to the river brought his heart to a standstill. A real fear took hold when the mare tucked her hind legs underneath her body, desperately trying to slow herself down. Stones dislodged from the gravely slope, rolled dangerously close as man and horse tumbled into the river with an enormous splash.

CHAPTER 4

Learning About Life

THE THIRD TIME Jerry Beaumont looked back, there was still no one behind him. He pulled his horse up and turned it around. Afraid and angry with himself for ever allowing it to happen, his mind raced with thoughts of the consequences, if he had gone straight instead of following him left along the trail. Hoping for his friend to suddenly appear, Jerry urged his horse on. However, the closer he came to the trail's junction without any sign of Nick, the more certain he was of disaster.

At the junction he galloped hard left, following the hoof marks of a fast-running horse that led down the path straight to the steep embankment. Dismounting, Jerry carefully walked to the sandy edge and peered over. Gravel and small stones clattered downwards, raining into the dark waters below. The evidence of a massive struggle all the way down the sandy embankment was clear, but there was no trace of Nick or the horse. Frantic, Jerry ran along the edge of the steep incline, eyes searching the water for any sign of a floating body.

He had gone several hundred yards when from somewhere in the bush, he heard the faint sound of what seemed like someone whistling. Standing still, he listened and after a few seconds the sound came again. Following in the direction from where he was sure it had come, he made his way around several small stands of trees and large boulders. All at once the whistling started again; this time it sounded as though it was no more than a few yards away. Stepping out from behind a large rock, a butt-naked Nick Roberts smiled and said: "I guess you win."

"What in the name of thunder...!" Jerry looked around at the wet clothes spread across the rocks. "And where's your horse? Is the old girl okay?"

"She's fine, just a few scrapes, like me," Nick replied, pointing across the clearing to where the horse was grazing. Then, stacking more twigs onto the pile of dried grass and leaves he asked: "Got a match?"

Jerry tossed a small waterproof metal cylinder filled with wooden matches. "That'll take forever," he said looking at the clothes on the rocks slowly drying in the fall sun. "I'll cut a stick to hang your clothing over the fire." He was back in a few minutes and walked to where Nick was huddled next to the now roaring fire. The self-conscious Jerry never looked down as he handed Nick a long stick. "I ain't waitin' around for you to get that ugly butt of yours covered. Besides, I gotta find my horse." And he was gone, and Nick rubbed the excruciating pain in his shoulder.

Friday morning, an anxious Nick Roberts had been pacing about at the road turnoff for some time, when Miranda drove up with the children. He rushed to open her door and greeted each of them with an enthusiastic hello.

Joseph had the day off from school, so they would be spending three days with him. To Miranda's surprise, Joseph had been eager to return to the wilderness, and immediately made Nick promise to take him fishing.

From the trunk of her car, Nick removed a small metal stove she loan him and carried it to where the horse was tied. Together with the new piping, he secured the stove to the travois. With the children atop the horse, they set off for the camp.

Nick's plan was to take them to a nearby mountain for a day of hiking and sightseeing. It was a long and tiring walk, especially for two small children, so Nick attached the travois to the horse and placed the knapsack on it. As soon as he unloaded the stove and Miranda stored her parcels in the tepee, they began making their way up the long trail. A few hundred feet up, they spotted several white mountain-goats on rock ledges far above. As they stood there, craning to get a look, high in the sky a golden eagle, its giant wings shifting side to side, glided and soared in a circle until suddenly it plunged straight towards the valley floor. Only a few feet above the ground, the huge eagle sped across the green grass and a split second later, deadly talons gripped the fleeing rabbit.

Nick explained to the children how catching the rabbit was

nature's way of control. "Only the strongest, fastest, and the smartest, of a species survive. And that's good for everyone."

After a brief rest, they continued the climb, moving single file up the mountainside. They had been walking for only a short while when they came across a small flock of sheep. The four mature females, with two small lambs at their side, were acting strange, nervously milling about, bleating loud. For some reason, they were very distressed and reluctant to leave the edge of a deep crevice even with the approach of humans.

When they got closer to the edge, Joseph pointed to something moving far below in the gully. After staring down for a moment, Nick realized it was a large ram and understood the reason for the other lambs' anxiety.

"It's a ram. He must have fallen in and got trapped in the crevice with no way out."

"What's a ram?" Leah asked, clutching Nick's sleeve and peering down.

"That's a male lamb, Leah. And that's his family."

"Can you get him out?" Leah's voice echoed both the child's fear and her sadness.

"I'm not sure, but we can certainly try," Nick assured her, moving to unhitch the travois. Falling down a cliff was something he knew little about, Nick laughed to himself as he tied the long rope around his waist. After looping the other end around the horse's chest, he backed it to the edge of the gully then explained to Miranda she would have to inch the horse slowly forward in order to bring him back up.

Miranda gripped the halter, steadying the horse, while Nick lowered himself hand-over-hand down the slope to where he could get close enough to grasp the ram by its horns. Out of fear, the animal struggled to get away from him but he finally managed to get a secure grip. He signaled to Miranda who eased the horse away from the cliff, pulling Nick and the ram up to the top.

As soon as the ram's feet touched solid ground, it took off like lightning. "There's another one wedged in the crevice even further down. It seems likely the two of them had been fighting over the females and they fell over the edge," Nick said moving the horse back and lowering himself down again. This time, Nick found that the animal was wedged in between rocks at a point

Rescuing the ram from the crevice.

where he could barely reach it. He made a loop in the rope and managed to get it around one of the ram's back legs and as Miranda pulled him up he did his best to hold the animal away from the sharp rocks.

When they made it to the top of the cliff, the ram's eyes were open but it couldn't move. Its back was broken and the animal was suffering. Nick knew that if they left it there, sooner or later a bear would get it, or it would die an agonizing death from starvation. Either way, it had to be put down. Without a gun, the most humane thing to do was to quickly end its suffering with a blow from a large rock.

"Take the children out of sight," he told Miranda. "This is something I don't want them to see at their age."

When it was over, Nick called out and Miranda and the children returned. "It won't go to waste," Nick said and Miranda volunteered to apply her newfound skills to help dress the ram. By the time they finished, two tired children were anxious to go home. Loading the carcass on the travois, they headed back to camp.

Nick had a lot of moose meat in the smokehouse and on the drying racks. Most of the mutton would go in the hole he had dug into the permafrost where it would freeze. The hide was blood-soaked and covered with mud from the ram's battle but there were no holes in it. When Nick cleaned it up and started the tanning process, he was pleased to see it was in pretty good shape. The wool would provide an additional warm cover for sleeping in the cold nights ahead.

Nick set up the stove in the middle of the tepee while Miranda set about preparing dinner. The children, sent to fetch a pail of water from the stream, returned soaking wet and the pail less than half full. But Miranda couldn't be upset, they were laughing and playful in a way she had not seen for a long time.

Lamb chops and baked potatoes were on the menu, the last meal to be cooked outdoors for a while. After finishing supper, Leah, who had watched Joseph help Nick the last time, wanted to share in the dish washing. Not to be left out, Joseph immediately said he would do the drying. Nick found a block of wood just the right height so Leah could reach the dishpan on the makeshift table and as they worked, Nick told them a story.

With the dishes done, Nick lit a fire in the new stove then helped tuck two tired children into bed. Within seconds, both asked for another story.

"How about if your mother told us all a story," Nick replied.

"Nick, you tell them another one. I don't know any, and you're better at it than I am." Miranda shook her head.

"You must remember at least one story from when you were a child," Nick coaxed.

"Well, okay. I do remember one story. Once upon a time there were three bears. A mama bear, a papa bear, and a baby bear," Miranda began.

"Aw, we've heard that one a hundred times, Mom. Tell us a new one!" Leah interrupted.

"I don't know any others well enough to retell them," Miranda said, blushing.

"Nick, would you tell us another one?" Leah pleaded.

"Another night I will, but tonight I have some personal things that I have to get done."

Joseph and Leah lay back on their pillows and quickly fell asleep. Miranda and Nick stayed up for a while, talking only sporadically as he busied himself with paperwork. She told him that it had been a long time since she had seen her children as happy or as relaxed as they were out here in the bush with him. "They have never had anyone pay so much attention to them. Being here has been awfully good for them — and for me. Thank you, Nick."

"It goes both ways, Miranda. I've enjoyed every minute, myself. You guys are welcome to spend as much time here as you want." He set his paperwork aside then remembering, said: "Would you mind taking this back with you and getting it in the mail right away?"

"Of course, Nick. I'll mail it first thing when I get home." She looked straight at him, assessing his face to see his reply when she asked: "Are you sure you don't mind having the three of us around?"

"Not at all! The children remind me so much of myself at that age, asking questions and always wanting to hear stories. Actually," a bashful Nick looked away, "it gets pretty lonely around here when you guys are gone. It would be nice if we could all spend the winter out here together."

I've been thinking about that during the last few days," Miranda said firmly. "Joseph is learning more out here in the bush with you than he has ever learned in school. Not that it's the school's fault; it's his behavior that causes the problems. This year I had thought about teaching him his grade two at home, and since Leah has not started school yet, there would be no problem with her if we were living out here. My wildlife biology course is by correspondence through the Yukon College. That means I too can study out here. If you are sure you can put up with us, I'll talk to the kids in the morning and see what they think."

They continued to discuss the idea and Miranda explained that lately Joseph had been getting into more and more trouble at school. "The white kids tease him about being Indian, and he gets mad and punches one of them. Then, they all gang up on him and of course he ends up in trouble with the teachers for hitting first and being disruptive. Joseph feels that everyone in the world is against him, and he's starting to rebel against everything. It just keeps getting worse all the time. The angrier he gets, the more they tease him."

"Bullying can be real tough for a kid that age," Nick shook his head in disgust.

"It's gotten so bad that Joseph is playing hooky from school. I tried walking with him to the front door and making sure he went in but later I learned he was going in one door and straight out the back. Then he would spend all day goofing off down by the river."

"That's serious," Nick looked pensive.

"Joseph is missing a father, Nick. But, it's easy to see he's getting to like and trust you. I see the time you take with him, even showing him the different types of trees, their bark and leaves, and all the various types of grasses. You known, after you explained the different berries, where to find them, and which ones were good to eat? He was thrilled and at home, he talked about that and the other things constantly. He needs to know about living in the wilderness, about the plants and animals and all the ways of his ancestors. Both of the children could learn a lot from a winter here with you."

In the morning, it was windy and the rain was beating down on the tepee. Still rehashing their conversation over and over in his mind, Nick lit a fire in the stove, put the tea on, and started preparing porridge.

Leah was up first; she came over and sat next to him, wanting to help. Together they mixed some powdered milk, set out four bowls, then called Miranda and Joseph for breakfast.

As they ate, Miranda asked the children if they would like to spend the winter out here in the wilderness with Nick. Leah's eyes lit up like candles, and she was almost shouting when she spoke. "Yes! Yes! I want to stay out here all the time. I never want to go back home."

Joseph, on the other hand, had a worried look on his face. "If it means I don't have to go back to that school, then I'm all for it."

Miranda said she would teach him his grade two but he would have to go back to school in the spring to write his exams.

"Nick, are you sure you could put up with the three of us all winter?" Miranda asked, still uncertain.

"It's not me putting up with the three of you. It's all four of us putting up with each other, and yes, with a little effort, I think we can do it."

"Okay, then it's settled. I'll make the arrangements for Joseph's schooling and my biology course."

Miranda Delaney and her children had grown up in a white man's world, one filled with conveniences. Inside plumbing, electricity, refrigerators and microwave ovens, plus all the other things that had become necessities were just an accepted part of everyday life. And the children were going to a white man's school, learning nothing of their heritage other than the little they had garnered from a few school outings. Miranda had never been able to teach her children anything about the land or their people and they were growing up knowing almost nothing of the old Indian customs, how their ancestors survived in the wilderness, or how they had lived in harmony with nature for thousands of years before the white man arrived.

There was something missing in their lives. They weren't quite sure exactly what it was but Miranda knew her children could never completely fit into a world they didn't understand. She thought that if her children could learn something about their ancestors and how they had lived, only then could they fit into the world they were living in today.

There was also something missing in Miranda's life. Something she had been searching for ever since her husband died. It was more than just the companionship of a man, or even the bond of a family relationship, there was a void in her existence that all too often left her laying awake in bed until late at night. Raising two children alone was difficult, and the small annual income from the money invested from the proceeds of her husband's life insurance policy, meant pinching pennies and constantly worrying about expenses. Taking her wildlife biology course helped give her hope for the day far down the road when she could use a degree to get a good job. For now, she needed to sort through all those feelings and at least try to determine what she could do about filling the emptiness in her life.

Even though he was a white man, Miranda knew and appreciated the skills and knowledge Nick Roberts possessed about the old Indian ways. And, despite not having children, he also knew a lot about getting along with them. Always happy, always with a ready laugh, Nick Roberts was fun to be around. Although a big, powerful man, he had a gentleness about him that made her feel safe and at ease whenever they were together, even deep in the woods. For her children, Nick took the time to explain things the way the Indians had taught him. In his whole life, he had told her one time, he had never found anything else that made as much sense.

CHAPTER 5

Preparing for Winter

WINTER WAS FAST APPROACHING. If they were to stay in the woods, they would have to take stock of everything they had on hand to determine what would be needed to sustain four people in the wilderness for six months. Once the winter snows started falling, their vehicles would be snowed in and the only way out would be a minimum three-day trek on snowshoes to Carmacks.

Nick already had on hand an axe, a bucksaw, a file, two rolls of haywire, a pair of pliers, wire cutters, a hammer, and some nails of various sizes. But, they would need an extra axe, four or five more rolls of haywire, some snare wire, another file, several pounds of nails plus eight-inch spikes, two galvanized water buckets, and a tub for heating water on the stove.

At present, the food supply consisted of approximately four hundred and fifty pounds of moose meat, of which one hundred and fifty pounds was dried and the remainder frozen in the permafrost along with ninety pounds of mutton. He had almost one hundred pounds of salmon left; some smoked and some dried. It all worked out to just a little less than one pound of meat per person, per day. If they could supplement that with a few rabbits or ptarmigan, they would have enough meat to last the winter. Nick spent a lot of time preparing a list of the various supplies they would have to buy. Needing to make sure he thought of everything and that each was bought in adequate quantity, he wrote it down.

He would also have to pick up a hundred and twenty-five bails of hay for the horse. Even though the outfitter had said he could use the horse for as long as he wanted, Nick felt it only proper to stop by the man's place and let him know what was happening. Hopefully too, the outfitter would be able to tell him where he

Nick's Supply List

200 lbs. flour	10 lbs. oatmeal
25 lbs. salt	4 boxes cream of wheat
30 lbs. sugar	cereal
20 lbs. butter	10 boxes dried bran cereal
25 lbs. rice	2 boxes shredded wheat
25 lbs. dried beans	3 cases toilet paper
10 lbs. dried peas	25 gal. lamp oil
250 lbs. potatoes	5 roles snare wire
15 lbs. carrots	24 bars hand soap
5 lbs. turnips	6 shampoo & conditioner
5 lbs. beets	15 spools thread
5 lbs. parsnip	(different sizes and colors)
2 gal. cooking oil	5 boxes wooden matches
4 lbs. tea	20 lbs. laundry detergent
6 boxes chocolate bars	6 dish soap
5 lbs. hard candy	extra gauze and tape for the
2 tins cocoa	first aid kit
20 lbs. powdered milk	toothache drops

could purchase some hay in the Carmacks area. With a bit of luck, there might be some available, if not, it would mean bringing a load all the way from Whitehorse.

While Miranda and Leah reviewed the supply list, Joseph told Nick about a sweat lodge that his grandfather had described in great detail to him just before he died. "Grandfather said the sweat lodge was a sacred place where you go to clean your body, mind, and soul!"

Nick almost laughed at the grown-up words coming from the mouth of the very serious seven-year-old.

Joseph then asked Nick if he knew how to build a sweat lodge, and if he would help build one, someday. Nick told the boy he hadn't been inside one for many years, but thought he could still remember how they were built. He said having one sounded like a great idea, but if they wanted one to use this winter they would have to start on it right away.

Nick talked to Miranda and they agreed she should go to Carmacks ahead of time to prepare things. Joseph asked to stay with Nick, and Miranda agreed. She and Leah left early the next morning, Nick and Joseph walking with them to her vehicle.

Back at the campsite, Nick and Joseph began preparations for the sweat lodge by going to the swamp and chopping down fifty alder poles. They selected only those that were about four inches in diameter and could be cut into six-foot lengths. Using the horse, they hauled the heavy poles to the campsite and stacked them close to the tepee. The rest of the first day was spent sharpening one end of each pole and then hammering them a few inches into the soft ground in a semicircular pattern leaving only enough space for a doorway.

On their second day, they placed five logs across the top of the structure and wove branches under and over until the roof was fully covered. Atop this, they spread swamp grass and covered the entire surface area with sod to make a waterproof roof. Inside the small structure, they built benches along two of the walls. To seal the doorway to the new sweat lodge they used a piece of heavy canvas.

It had proven to be much more work than Nick had anticipated and after completing the construction, he was tired and eager to try it out. From the stream he and Joseph filled two large pails with water; from the stream's edge they gathered two dozen rocks, each between six to eight inches in diameter. Carrying the heavy rocks, they had to make several trips to the nearby campsite and when done they built a large bonfire and heated the rocks. Two four-foot-long sticks were wrapped with haywire about a foot from the ends, keeping them apart. They used this contraption to lift the hot rocks out of the fire and to place them in the back of the sweat lodge.

Nick told Joseph to get changed while he organized the rocks. A short time later, wrapped in a towel, Joseph raced inside the sweat lodge. Nick went to the tepee, changed, and brought back two mats.

Joseph didn't seem very enthused with the sweat lodge until Nick poured the cold water over the hot rocks, producing instant steam. Before long, the small room heated up so much they had to pour the remaining water over themselves.

As they relaxed in the sweltering steam, Joseph said that his grandfather had told him that in a sweat lodge they sang songs to Mother Earth, to the sky, and to all the animals that had given their lives so they would have food and clothing.

This time the boys grown-up words brought an open laugh from Nick, and he quipped about his singing, telling Joseph he had a voice that would do nothing but drive the animals away in horror.

For a while they relaxed, saying nothing until Joseph began talking about school. He said he hated the boys in his school for teasing and fighting with him and he hated the teachers for blaming him for starting fights.

Nick explained that when he was a young boy, he too had gone through something similar. "What I learned, Joseph, was not to hate your enemies. If you do, that hatred will destroy you. An elderly Indian taught me that and what he told me stayed with me forever. I can remember his words as though it were yesterday. He said 'respect your enemies for what they are, learn all their weaknesses, but also learn what makes them strong. Only then can you live in harmony with them. Do not hate anyone or anything. Hate will torment you; it will make you lonely and you'll grow old before your time. Only love will give you peace and contentment. Love will lighten your heart and lighten your load as you go through life. It will bring you many friends, and your enemies will all disappear. You will gain much respect, and every step you take through life will be a little easier'."

Joseph listened with great intensity. Then, with a puzzled look on his face, asked, "How will all my enemies disappear?"

Nick thought for a moment, hoping he could explain it properly. "Some will become friends. Some will respect your territory and stay clear. And others, if you put them out of your mind, will just fade away."

"You know what? You think you sing bad?" Joseph abruptly changed the subject. "Well, my little sister says I sing pretty awful, too. But I don't care." and the boy broke into a memorized song.

Nick listened for a little then joined in as best he could. In a sweat lodge in the wilderness, far from any listening ears, he quickly gained his courage and began belting it out. They had been wailing their songs to the Great Spirit and to Mother Earth for almost twenty minutes when all at once raucous laughter echoed through the walls of the sweat lodge. The singing came to an abrupt halt, but Miranda and Leah's laughter did not. When the women peeked inside the sweat lodge they laughed even more at the embarrassed men.

When they came outside, the teasing continued until Joseph turned to his mother and said: "When you and Leah go in and sing songs to Mother Earth, the Great Spirit won't laugh at you, but he will clean your body, your mind, and your soul."

"My body sure needs a good cleaning. And it wouldn't hurt to cleanse my mind and soul at the same time," Miranda laughed lightly. "I think us ladies should take a turn."

After reheating the rocks and placing them back in the sweat lodge with two more pails of water, Nick and Joseph waited inside the tepee while Miranda and Leah tried it out. Within a few minutes, they could hear female voices but the steam bath had made Nick and young Joseph almost lethargic and they soon drifted off to sleep. When they woke more than an hour later, the delicious aroma of Miranda's cooking filled the tepee.

After dinner, while Miranda was gathering whatever they needed for the next day's trip to Carmacks, Nick told the children a story about a squirrel that all the other animals laughed at.

"The squirrel was busy scampering back and forth gathering nuts and acorns for the long winter ahead when a rabbit called out to him, *Hey, Mr. Squirrel, come and play hide-and-seek with us.* The rabbit, a crow, and a fox were running about playing and laughing. They wanted the squirrel to join in, but the squirrel replied: *No, I don't have time to play hide-and-seek. I have to gather nuts and acorns for the winter.* But the rabbit was quick to reply: *you can gather them up anytime. Come play with us now and we'll help you gather nuts and acorns later.* But the little squirrel paid no attention and went about his work. The rabbit, the crow, and the fox sat on a log laughing and making fun of him. The crow said, *Squirrel, you work too hard and don't have any fun. If you come and play with us, you would find out that it's much better than working all day.* But the squirrel just kept on working. When winter arrived it was very long and cold, and there was no food to be found anywhere. All the animals were very hungry, except for the little squirrel. When the others asked the squirrel for some of his nuts and acorns, he told them he had only enough for himself and his family for the winter. If they had been gathering food instead of playing hide-and-seek all day, they would have food for themselves and their families, too. And so, to this day, no animal ever laughs at any squirrel as it scurries about gathering nuts and acorns instead of playing with all the other animals."

Miranda prepared hot cocoa and before long Leah and Joseph were nodding off. Nick helped tuck the children into bed without waking them.

Chapter 6

The Trip for Supplies

B Y SUNRISE the next morning they were all heading for town. Nick and Miranda rode on the horse, while Joseph and Leah sat on the travois. At the turnoff, where their vehicles were parked, Nick made preparations so he could leave the horse tethered to a twenty-foot rope for the few days they would be gone. The rope was tied to a ring, which in turn was placed around another seventy-foot rope pegged to the ground at each end. Tying the horse in this manner allowed it to graze a strip of grass forty feet wide by one hundred and ten feet long while letting it reach the brook for fresh water.

In Nick's pickup truck, Joseph sat in the middle while Leah sat on Miranda's knees. The road to Carmacks was rough gravel and filled with potholes. They needed nearly three hours to cover the more than sixty miles to town. When they arrived, Nick dropped off Miranda and the children at their home and immediately headed for the city of Whitehorse. More than a 200-mile return trip, he did not relish the drive but had no real choice in the matter. Although Whitehorse had a population of only twenty-two thousand people, it did have a variety of stores where he would be able purchase everything they needed.

While there, he made a brief stop to say hello to Cliff and Virginia, the friends at whose place he'd stayed when he first came to the Yukon. He thought Cliff would probably have extra hay to sell due to the sprinkler system he'd installed in the field the year before that had doubled his hay production.

Nick pulled into the ranch at about twelve-thirty in the afternoon just as Cliff and Virginia were finishing lunch. Nick joined them for a cup of tea from the large percolator that was always kept on the counter. When he told them of his plans to spend the winter in the Nisling Valley, they both said he was nuts but thought it would indeed be a great experience. Cliff had all the hay Nick needed and because the next day he and his wife had to drive through Carmacks on their way to Faro, they would gladly drop the load off on the way through.

It was past two o'clock by the time Nick left the ranch and headed to Whitehorse. There, he stopped at a clothing store and bought a heavy winter sweater. For whatever reason he suddenly decided to buy Miranda a dark green turtleneck sweater and as a second thought, added a pair of blue jeans. He didn't know why he bought them, or if he would ever give them to her, but it just felt like a nice thing to do at the time.

It was dark by the time he pulled into Carmacks with his large load of groceries and supplies. Miranda was still waiting up for him. She'd kept his supper hot in the oven, and had made up a bed for him on the living room sofa.

In the morning, despite the bright sunshine, it was quite cold out and a thick frost covered Miranda's front lawn. He knew they were pushing their luck, this time of year in the Yukon a heavy snowfall could happen anytime.

Miranda prepared a few things she and the children would need for the next few days and the rest of their clothing and personal items she packed in boxes. With Nick's truck nearly full, he would come back for the boxes when he returned to Carmacks to pick up the hay.

By ten o'clock they were loaded and headed for the woods. When the truck pulled into the cut-off, the horse looked up and trotted towards them. Nick stepped out, slipped his hand in his pocket, and gave the horse a treat.

For the children, it would be a long walk to the camp but with so much to bring they had no real choice. They managed to load a little less than half of the supplies on the horse's back and on the travois, making sure that on this first trip they brought the fresh vegetables and anything else that might freeze if left overnight. After walking for about five minutes, little Leah tired and traveled the rest of the way to the camp on Nick's shoulder.

As soon as the supplies were unloaded, Nick told Miranda that he would go back for another load right away rather than wait for the morning. "I'm just too worried about a snow storm coming in," he told her, scanning the skyline.

The second trip didn't take long as Nick filled the travois with supplies and rode on the horse. When he opened the flap to the tepee and stepped inside, a well-organized Miranda had already put everything away and was preparing a late supper.

"So, were you able to get everything?" she asked.

"Almost, but I'll finish it all first thing in the morning—unless we get a heavy snowfall, then I'll have to make several trips. But, it's the hay I'm really worried about." Any time now, there would be deep snow, making the roads impassable. He had to get all the hay into camp or they would have to give up on the idea of spending the winter here.

"Hungry?"

"Starved," he said reaching out to accept the plate of steaming hot food.

The following morning Nick headed out early for Carmacks to get the bales of hay. While waiting for Cliff to show up, he drove to Miranda's house to pick up her boxes of personal things. She had arranged for a neighbor to check on her place regularly, but he turned off the water and drained the pipes, just in case.

As the day wore on, an anxious Nick watched the highway for Cliff's truck. By mid afternoon he was certain something was wrong. It was almost seven o'clock in the evening and already dark when Cliff drove into the village with the load of hay. Apologizing profusely for being so late, he told Nick that his old truck had broken down on the highway.

As quickly as possible they unloaded the hay bales in Miranda's driveway and Nick rushed to stack as many as possible on his truck. After saying good-bye to Cliff, he threw a canvas over the top of the hay, tied it down, and headed back to camp. It was well past midnight when a tired Nick Roberts was greeted by a worried Miranda.

It was the morning of November 2nd, a day Nick Roberts would remember for the rest of his life. A week had gone by since they'd brought in their first supplies and today a greatly relieved Nick would be going into town to pick up the last load of hay.

As usual, his day began before sunrise and one where the outside temperature had dropped to five degrees below zero. This kind of cold was still bearable but a gusting thirty-mile-per hour northeast wind made things much more frigid. On horseback, he had gone only a few yards from the tepee when following the trail to the truck became nearly impossible. The swirling snow, driven by an ever-increasing strong wind, was blinding him. Although he had the trees blazed along the trail through the bush, when he hit the open prairie it was a total whiteout. He let the horse have free rein, allowing its sense of direction from the many prior trips to lead them to where he had parked the truck. Safely there, he unhooked the travois and led the horse to the brook for a drink of water. He then tied her to a tree and, because the snow was so deep that it made grazing impossible, he removed the bale of hay from the back of his pickup. The one bale, left there for just such a purpose, he broke in two. He put one half out for the horse, the other half he set outside of the horse's walking range. If he left her any water it would freeze, so to quench her thirst she would have to eat snow.

The road into Carmacks was covered with snow, but it was the icy patches underneath that made the trip nerve-racking. It was slow motoring the entire way and the truck had to be in four-wheel drive at all times. When Nick finally arrived in the village, he headed straight for the small café and a relaxing cup of tea. At the grocery store he bought four heads of lettuce and some tomatoes for their last green salads until spring. For a moment he stopped, thinking about what that really meant.

They had plenty of powdered milk but as an afterthought, he bought six one-gallon jugs of milk that they could freeze. Then, he loaded the last of the bales of hay on his truck and headed back to camp.

He hoped the weather would have improved, but it only worsened. The road was getting harder to follow because the drifting snow made the visibility almost zero. About halfway home, he was inching his truck through a whiteout when he hit an icy patch and slid into the ditch. Thankfully, the truck remained level and the hay load did not spill but he needed more than an hour to get the truck shoveled out and back onto the road.

Darkness was beginning to settle in when he arrived at the cut-off. The horse was standing below the long boughs of a pine tree but the half bale of hay he had left near the parking spot was gone. "Deer," he thought, knowing the hay could not have been reached by the tethered horse. In the bitter cold it took longer than usual to hook up the travois and tie some of the hay bales onto it and the horse's back. By the time he finished, his fingers were numb. At least though, the snow had lessened and the wind had died down considerably—- for now.

Nick led the horse through the first grove of trees and was about a hundred yards into a wide clearing when he saw the herd of wood buffalo directly in front of him. Startled, he was immediately cautious because he knew wood buffalo had a reputation for sometimes being dangerous. About twice the size of their cousin the prairie buffalo, a large bull could weigh as much as three thousand pounds.

Nick turned and was heading south to go around them when all of a sudden two of the large animals broke away from the herd and started galloping towards him. Fear gripped the pit of his stomach and he could feel the hair rise on the back of his neck. He knew his only chance would be to get away from open ground and back into the thick bush. He reversed direction, instantly breaking into a run. Halfway to the bush he glanced back and saw that the buffalo were gaining on him, fast. He let go of the horse and split to the right, running as hard as he could. The buffalo followed the horse until the travois started banging into trees and breaking up. But, first one of the huge buffaloes and then the second, stopped, changed direction, and then charged towards him.

Nick's quick glimpse back revealed one of the charging beasts was only a few yards back and in desperation he dodged behind a large cedar tree. He could have touched the animal as it stormed past. A second later the other buffalo caught him square in the back and all he felt was his body hurtling through the air — then everything went dark.

When he came to, he felt a warm breath on the side of his face. As his eyes slowly opened, he could see an outline of a large animal. Gripped with fear and unable to run away, he tried to roll over and cover his head. Again he felt the warm breath, as his eyes focused on the large object standing over him.

A horse, it's a horse he thought, one that had been running

Charging wood buffalo.

loose in the valley, one which he caught and used for months and hadn't even given it a name. "And now, as he looked up a name came to him, Angel! Angel is what he would call her from now on.

Nick struggled to his feet and as he did, he could feel blood running down his back. He was covered with snow but brushing it off would be too painful, so he gingerly stepped over to where he could reach out and hold onto the horse. He knew the travois was broken into pieces and the hay had been scattered all over the bush. Getting back to camp before he froze to death was foremost on his mind. He had no idea how long he had been unconscious and was suddenly worried about Miranda and the children being alone in the tepee.

Weak, he was unable to climb on the horse's back. After three or four tries he had to sit back down on the ground to gather his strength. He wanted to lay down again for a short rest, but an inner sense warned of the danger of freezing to death if he passed out. Determined, he got back up, and, wrapping an arm around the horse's neck, he urged the horse slowly along until he came to a tree stump. Exhausted from the effort, he leaned against its powerful neck then through sheer willpower climbed onto the stump and slid on the horse's back. He leaned forward and whispered: "Angel, take me home."

Miranda Delaney thought she heard a noise outside the tepee. A little nervous, she opened the flap and peered out, hesitated, then screamed at the sight of the lifeless figure slumped over on the horse. She touched Nick's leg and he moaned, but when she tried to help him off the horse, he cried out, gasping at the words that she should go easy.

With his full weight against her, it took all of Miranda's strength to get him inside and onto the bed. In the brightly lit tepee, her worried expression turned to outright horror when she removed his parka and saw the blood-caked flannel shirt.

"I'll be okay," he said, still struggling to speak above a whisper. "It's not as bad as it looks. Please take care of the horse first. She needs warm water and hay."

"Don't worry, Nick. I'll take care of the horse," young Joseph spoke up, trying to sound very manly. Leah remained sitting on the edge of her bed watching, the trauma the child felt, clearly visible in her face.

Careful Miranda ease Nick's shirt off, and laid him across the bed on his stomach. From the pot of water always kept warm on the stove, she poured some into a wash pan and dropped in a cloth to soak. She delicately patted the bloodied area on his back, cleaning until the deep wound was clearly visible. "Nick, you will have to see a doctor," she shook her head. "The wound are very deep and four or five inches long."

"I guess it wasn't my time," he mumbled.

"I'll dress it, and try draw out any poison that's in there."

"Thanks," his voice sounded a shade stronger. "I'm tired, I think..." he fell sleep.

Miranda set about dressing the wound. She applied honey over the gash then lay washed cabbage leaves over top, all of which she protected with an outer layer of gauze wrapped around his back. She knew there was a risk that the wound might develop an infection, and she would have to get him out of here and to a doctor. Covering Nick with a blanket, she dimmed the lamps and went to sit beside her still frightened daughter.

In the morning, she had hot tea ready and he seemed much better, sitting up with one part of his backside resting against a soft pillow. A proud Miranda listened as Joseph informed Nick that he had been up very early and had already fed and watered the horse.

Nick told them about the buffalo charging him and how the frightened horse stayed around, saving his life. "If she'd run off, I would never have gotten back here. That's why I've decided to call her Angel," he smiled at Leah.

He spent the next two days in the tepee but by the third day was able to get out and help gather wood. Joseph did as much splitting as he could, surprising Nick with his ability with an axe. Miranda wouldn't let Nick use the axe at all or do any strenuous work. Resigned to the fact that he did have to take it easy, he watched as Joseph did as much wood splitting as he could.

After a week's recuperation, Nick and Joseph rode Angel to the spot where they'd had the buffalo encounter. The travois was scattered in several pieces and its cargo of hay had been quickly devoured by the buffalo herd. Along with the hay, the buffalo had feasted on his heads of lettuce but Nick was grateful to find all six jugs of the frozen milk.

They went on to check out the rest of the hay bales still loaded on his truck. Despite the amount of lost hay, they would however have enough to get through the winter, barely. For now he was pretty certain the remaining hay was safe as it appeared that the buffalo herd had traveled in the opposite direction of his truck. Nonetheless, he knew they could roam back this way at anytime so building a new travois and getting the rest of the hay became a priority, regardless of the soreness he still felt from his injuries.

CHAPTER 7

Building the Corral

A NEW TRAVOIS was put together in record time and Nick was immensely pleased with the effort young Joseph had made to help. They had brought all the remaining hay safely to the campsite and under canvas cover when they discovered that the herd of wood buffalo was hanging around less than a mile east of their camp. There was no doubt the herd would eventually make their way to the haystack and Nick knew that if the buffalo got into the hay, not only would they eat most of it, but they would also trample a great deal into the ground. When finished, there wouldn't be enough hay left to feed the horse through the winter. The physical labor to survive here was turning out to be more than he had anticipated because now he would have to build a corral around the haystack to keep the buffalo out.

They got at it first thing the following morning and although it was very cold, the absence of wind made it relatively comfortable to work outside. Miranda, Leah, and Joseph all worked to build the corral, doing everything to minimize the hard labor for Nick. Nevertheless, he cut down forty-two poles, each from twelve to fifteen feet long. Miranda used the horse to haul the poles from the bush to the where they had stacked the hay. On each trip, the children came with her, riding on the horse's back. They worked only half of the day after Miranda insisted Nick not overdo it. Although he would never admit it, he was dead tired but pleased as most of the hard work was done. Finishing the corral the next day would be easy.

Up early, Nick was outside while the others still slept. He prepared each pole for use as a rail by notching the ends with an axe then lay them out on the ground in the spots where they were to be used. Hungry from the hard work, he was pleased when Miranda called him to breakfast. After their meal, they all came out to help.

Joseph held poles in place while Miranda nailed them to the outside of the trees. Nailing them in this manner, any buffalo leaning against them in an attempt to reach the hay couldn't knock the rails off. Within a few hours, the corral was complete and Nick breathed a sigh of relief that the horse's supply of hay was safe.

During lunch Nick had an idea and turned to Joseph. "Have you ever hunted with a bow and arrow?"

"No, but I have with a slingshot," he said proudly.

"He's really good," Miranda piped in. "He sets tin cans on the fence behind the house and can knock them off from quite a distance."

"Well, you're better than me, then. I couldn't hit the broad side of a barn with a slingshot," Nick laughed.

"I'll teach you!" Joseph fairly burst with pride. All of a sudden his face clouded. "Mom? Where did you pack my slingshot?"

Miranda pointed to the box at the foot of Joseph's cot.

"I have a whole pail of perfect-sized stones somewhere. Did you see them?" Joseph asked of his mother again, retrieving his slingshot to show Nick.

"I'd planned on doing some bow hunting," Nick said. "Joseph, would you like to help me make a hunting bow? If you want, we can make two."

The boy's eyes lit up.

That afternoon the two of them walked along the gully looking for cedar branches, Joseph with his slingshot tucked in his back pocket. Any bow suitable for hunting had to have enough moisture in it so that when pulled back, it wouldn't break, yet dry enough to fire an arrow a great distance. The first piece of wood Nick tried proved to be too wet. It bent but didn't spring back. The next one was too dry and it snapped in two. They tried over a dozen branches before finding two that were just right.

With darkness fast approaching they would have to hurry to find dry cedar to make the arrows. A wind was blowing from the east and the clouds were being whipped along by the strong winds aloft. With the possibility of a storm, they decided to head back to camp.

Along the trail they came across a flock of ptarmigan bedding down for the night in a thick spruce grove. Nick whispered to

Joseph and the boy removed his slingshot from his back pocket, reached into his jacket and came out with a handful of marble-sized stones. Joseph moved stealthily into the trees and within a few minutes emerged, grinning ear to ear, and carrying two ptarmigan.

It was completely dark by the time Nick opened the flap to the tepee and a proud Joseph rushed inside to show his mother the ptarmigan.

"He shot them with his slingshot?" she questioned. "Tin cans on a fence is one thing, but real live ptarmigan... wow!"

"Your son is pretty amazing with that thing. I don't think I've ever known any man so talented, never mind a boy his age."

As soon as they finished dinner and washed the dishes, Joseph and Leah put their pajamas on and waited for Nick to tell them a story. But, by the time Nick was ready, Joseph was already fast asleep.

"It's been quite a day for him," Miranda beamed, tucking the sheets around her son.

Leah played quietly with one of her dolls while Nick and Miranda finished drinking their tea. They talked for a while, then decided to turn in early.

Nick lay in the dark, but with the dim lamp still on, through the privacy sheet surrounding her bed area he could see the silhouette of Miranda's slender body as she undressed for bed. A warmth surged through him and he had to turn away. Still though, images of her danced in his head. Every once in a while, from a certain way she looked at him or the seemingly spontaneous touch of her hand on his, she had stirred his passions. He was never certain that there was anything real, telling himself it was only his mind wishing it were so. But he understood that the age difference was very real, and felt a responsibility to take care of them. His thoughts turned to her children and how much Joseph had changed since he first met that rude little boy. Telling stories and teaching them as much as he could of what the Indians taught him so many years ago. He would never allow anything to disrupt that.

Outside, the air was cold and calm. Only the howling of a wolf pack in the distance occasionally broke the silence. One would start to howl in a very low tone, getting higher and higher until it was lost in silence. Then another one and another would join in, until the whole pack howled.

As he listened, he slowly drifted off to sleep. Suddenly there was someone at the door of the tepee.

"Anybody home?" a voice called out from just outside the tepee.

"Who could that be at this time of night?" Miranda whispered.

"It sounds like my friend Jerry Beaumont," Nick said. "Just a minute, I'll open the door for you."

Nick got up, slipped his trousers on, and untied the door.

"Come in and hurry so you don't let in the snow and the cold. How come you're wandering around out here so late at night?"

"It's not that late. It's only eight o'clock. I was at this end of my trap line and decided to come visit you. See if you were all still alive."

Miranda had her kimono on and was sitting at the table by the time Jerry sat down. He took off his hat and coat and sat himself by the heater. By then children were both sitting up, anxious to see who this stranger was and what he had to say. This was the first visitor they had since moving into the camp in the fall.

They all joined in the conversation, happy to have a new face around. Nick boiled some water and made hot chocolate for everyone. A large bowl of ptarmigan stew was heated and served to Jerry.

While everyone was talking and laughing, Jerry's face suddenly became solemn. With a look of concern he said, "Nick, I want to warn you about some bear traps that were left behind last fall by poachers. The poachers were involved in trading of bear parts and were either in jail and couldn't remove them or were too lazy. I've found three or four of them already, and I just about stepped in one a couple of days ago. Be careful walking along the bear paths or in small bluffs where the bears might be bedding down."

"I don't think they would've come this far north. We haven't found any yet, but we certainly will watch out for them," Nick reassured him.

It was well after midnight by the time everyone had finally fallen asleep.

Jerry arose early the next morning, eager to continue on his trek. Nick, Miranda, and the kids stood by the door waving goodbye as he disappeared into the bushes.

CHAPTER 8

Getting to Know Each Other

A S THE DAYS GREW SHORTER and the nights longer, they tried to get out of the tepee as much as possible. Almost every morning, if the weather wasn't too cold or windy, they would explore different areas of the woods. Nick would try to remember as much as he could about what the Indians had taught him and would pass it on to Joseph, Leah, and Miranda.

He told them that nature could be their best teacher of all. They would only have to look, listen, feel, or smell everything that was around them. They could gain more knowledge than all the schools in the world. Observing the sun and stars could guide them along their trails. Nature's sheer immensity could teach them to be humble. The winds that would carry the seeds far away from the trees, dropping them in new locations waiting for the spring rains to nourish them into new life, would teach them to be patience. The waters of the rivers and lakes that would carry their canoes great distances wound teach them about faraway places. The same waters would bring the mighty salmon and other fish right to their doorstep. Trees and grasses could teach them about living and dying and how the old must make way for the new. Observing the habits of animals could teach them how to look after one another. Some animals live in herds and others live solitary lives, getting together only to mate or to raise their young.

Looking puzzled, Leah asked, "How come every time we see an animal in the woods, it's running?"

Nick told her how a wise old Indian once explained it to him. He said, "When a deer wakes up in the forest, it has to be able to run faster than the fastest wolf or it will be killed and eaten. When a wolf wakes up in the forest, it has to run faster than the slowest deer or it will starve to death. So, no matter what you are, when you wake up in the forest you have to be able to run fast to survive."

Joseph was quiet and did very little talking. Sometimes it seemed as though he was in a world of his own. When Nick showed him things about the bush or the animals, it seemed that he couldn't head or didn't understand. However, when he across a similar situation he would always know what to do. Leah, on the other hand was spunky and talkative, knowing all the answers almost before you could ask the questions. Her eyes were big and bright and sparkled when she laughed. She had long shiny black hair, a slender build, always smiling and always inquisitive.

Miranda was a perfect combination of both her children. She stood tall and erect. She carried her chin high, and her square shoulders made an impression as she moved. She could be very shy at times, but when she talked, her eyes would shine and her face would light up with a very special glow. The smile on her face was broad. She had pride in the way she looked after her children. They were her life and she showed it.

She told of her life growing up on an Indian reservation and how she'd felt about white people looking down on her because she was Indian.

She explained that in the early days, Indian children were not allowed to go to white schools. Most of the Indian kids stayed home and didn't go to school at all. "My father was the one who wanted me to go to an Indian residential school," she told them. "He wanted me to have an education even if he felt it wasn't as good as I would have received had I been allowed to go to a white school."

"The nearest Indian residential school was in Whitehorse. I remember helping my father hook up the team of horses to the wagon and loading the supplies for the four-day journey to the school. I washed the few clothes I had and put them in a bag to take with me. My mother stayed home to look after my younger brother and sister. I remember my mother hugging me and crying because I would be gone for such a long time."

"As I walked from the wagon to the front gate of the residential school and up the wide steps, my heart pounded. I looked back at my father a hundred times hoping he would call me back, telling me I didn't have to go. But he just sat on the wagon watching me walk up the steps of the school with a sad look on his face. He wouldn't go into the school with me because he couldn't speak

Indian residential school at Spanish, Ontario as it stands today.

English and was too embarrassed and uncomfortable around white people."

"When I opened the door and peeked inside, I saw a lady sitting behind a desk in the hallway. The lady was dressed in black except for a hooded cape with a white collar and a white peak framing her face. That was the first time I had ever seen a nun. As soon as she noticed me peeking through the doorway, she called, 'Come in,' motioning with her hand at the same time. If it hadn't been for the pleasant smile on her face, I think I would have turned around and run. Instead, I slowly made my way towards her desk."

"When I got there, she pointed to a chair beside the desk and said, 'My name is Sister Marie. Please sit down and tell me what yours is."

"I hesitated for a while before sitting down. I wasn't quite sure of what to make of all of this. My mother had taught me how to speak English, but I wasn't very comfortable with it. I always thought in Indian first and then found the English words to coincide with what I was thinking. I was always slow to answer, until later on when I started thinking in English. When I finished answering all her questions, she rang a bell on her desk and soon another nun came over."

"Sister Marie said, 'Sister Gabriel, this is Miranda. She will be staying with us. Please take her upstairs to room 324, help her make her bed, and please show her around the residence."

"The school was a large three-story building. The classrooms, kitchen, and a large dining room with a big long table in the center filled the first floor. The second floor contained the office and the nuns' quarters. The third floor was where we lived. Each room contained four beds, so there wasn't much privacy. In the basement was a large wood-burning furnace, a laundry room, and a large sewing room."

"I remember how the girls stared at me when I walked into the bedroom. I was wearing a long dress down to my ankles with moccasins, and I had two long braids hanging down my back. The other two girls in the room were Indian, but they wore white people's clothes. Sister Gabriel said that she would try to find me some other clothes to wear."

"The next day they had me outfitted with a dress that came down to my knees, instead of my ankles, and a pair of brown shoes. That was the first time I had ever worn shoes, and it took me a while to get used to them. They were not as comfortable as moccasins. None of the things were new, but I liked them and felt more like everyone else at the school."

"It wasn't long before I had many friends. Most of the nuns were friendly and also very helpful. The food was not fancy, but I liked it. Every day of the week we would have something different. Occasionally we even had fresh fruit on the table. I remember one time when I was reaching across the table to get something, I accidentally knocked an orange out of the bowl. It rolled across the table and onto the floor. Sister Rose saw it and accused me of trying to steal the orange. She said that for punishment, I would have to work two hours a day for one week in the sewing room. I didn't mind working in the sewing room at all, but I was so embarrassed and upset for being wrongfully accused in front of all my friends."

"Although I liked almost everything about the school and the residence, I missed my family. At night I would pull the covers over my head, hoping no one would hear me crying. For a long time, I cried myself to sleep until one day it just stopped. I finally accepted the fact that this strange place was going to be my home for a long, long time."

"The loneliest time I had was spending the first Christmas at the residence. Almost everyone except the nuns went home for the holidays. There were only four of us girls left. The other three girls had no families and nowhere else to go. I had a family, but it was much too far to travel home in the winter. I remember a man coming to the residence with a parcel from my parents, just before Christmas. When I opened it up, there was a brand-new pair of moccasins, a fur cap, some dry smoked moose meat, and a rag doll that my mother had made. I still have that doll to this day. Soon the holidays were over and everything was back to normal."

"I became best friends with a girl named Gloria. She was one of the girls who didn't have any parents. She moved into the empty bed in my room so we could be closer. I found most of the girls in school to be friendly, but Gloria and I seemed to have something special. We always shared our most intimate secrets with each other."

"As soon as school was out for the summer, my father came to get me with a team of horses and a wagon. When we saw him coming down the road, Gloria and I ran out to meet him. I couldn't wait to ask him if Gloria could come home with us for the summer. He said we had enough room, and she was welcome to stay with us."

"That summer went by very fast. Gloria was happy to meet my family and all my friends. When the summer holidays were over, we were soon back in school and into the old routine. There were a lot of new girls in school that year, and I'm sure a lot of them were going through much the same thing as I did when I first got there. It wasn't long before they were playing and mixing with everyone else."

"The following year my brother, Peter, went to the boys' residential school. I went in with him and stayed for a while to help him get settled in. Then I went back to my school and unpacked my things. It was nice seeing all my friends again. Sister Marie had left due to health reasons. I liked her the best of all the nuns and knew I would miss her very much."

"The year after, my sister, Beth, started school. She wasn't allowed to stay in my room. She had to stay in a room with other grade ones, but I was always around to look after her. In the evenings, I would go to her room and read to her. I knew how lonely it had been for me that first year, and I wanted to make it easier for her."

"Another sad time for all of us was when I was in grade five. Just before Christmas, we received a sad message. It said that our mother had died three weeks before of tuberculosis. Due to the long distance and bad weather at that time of year, we couldn't even go home for the funeral. I remember crying myself to sleep every night for a long while because I knew I would never see her again. Two months later, we got another message that our father had passed away, also from TB. I guess he must have caught it when he was looking after my mother. The crying started all over again. Soon after that, my sister, brother, and I were taken to Whitehorse for chest X-rays. Fortunately, all our X-rays came back negative."

"That was the first time since the summer holidays that I had a chance to talk to my brother Peter. I knew he was having difficulty in school, but I had no idea how bad it really was. He told me how terrible the food was and that he never had enough to eat and was always hungry. He said he was forced to work long hours in the horse barn, tailor shop, and in the garden. He told me about him run away. He said that when they caught him, two of the priests held him across a table, while the third one beat him with a leather strap."

"When I got back to school, I told the nuns everything my brother had told me about going hungry and about the priests beating him. The nuns were shocked at the story and promised they would do something about it"

"About a week later, the nuns called me into the office and informed me that Indian Affairs was now conducting an investigation into the treatment and quality of food at the boys' residential school. They assured me that things would certainly get much better for my brother and the rest of the boys at the school. After that, our lives changed dramatically."

"The next summer when our uncle came to pick us up at the school, he had a tractor and freight wagon. I remember it was a long rough bumpy ride home, but we made it all the way in one day. Things were different at home now. Everywhere we went there was something that reminded us of our mother and father. It turned out to be a very long, sad summer."

"I was glad to get back to school that year. We didn't go back home for the next three years. Everyone felt it would be better for all of us to stay away from such sad memories. When we finally did go back home, it wasn't that bad after all. Just about everywhere we went, we found something that brought back wonderful memories of our parents. To this day, living in their tiny little house brings back nothing but good memories."

"Peter told me he was now enjoying the residential school. Soon after telling me the story, the government inspectors came in and got rid of the four priests that were the meanest. The priests that replaced them were much younger and had all the boys involved in sports. There was baseball and soccer in the summer, hockey and snowshoeing in the winter."

"With the appointment of Father Oliver as the new Father Superior, the changes were dramatic. There was less work in the barns, in the gardens, and in the tailor shop and more time spent in the classrooms. With the hiring of two additional qualified teachers, the school was upgraded to include Grades nine, ten, and eleven. The boys were no longer compelled to attend school. They attended because they enjoyed it and wanted to further their education."

CHAPTER 9

Winter's Moving In

E ACH DAY the temperature edged downwards and heavy snowfalls followed one on the other until the deep snow made walking anywhere nearly impossible without snowshoes. Nick knew that before long he would have to make at least one pair for himself to ensure he could gather firewood. Making snowshoes was something young Joseph very much wanted to learn and one morning he and Nick set out to obtain the wood needed. They waded through the deep snow along the riverbank heading to a place Nick had scouted out weeks earlier while hunting. The large clump of willows grew straight and there were plenty about two or three inches in diameter. They cut down four lengths and brought them back to camp.

On the stove they filled a tub with water and heated it to a boil. After squaring two twelve foot long willows to about one inch by one inch, Nick placed the middles of the squared-off willows over the steam. He showed Joseph how wood softened by the steam could be bent in different directions so that the front of the snowshoe could be made to curve upwards. He carved two flat pieces of wood for the front and back of each snowshoe to hold the frames apart.

While Nick and Joseph were busy with the wood, Miranda pitched in, cutting quarter inch strips from the moose hide. She went around and around with a sharp knife until she had created one strip of hide, over a hundred feet long. Finished, she watched as Nick tied a wire around a four-inch nail and held it in the fire until it was red-hot then used it to burn holes in the wood an inch and a half apart all the way around the wooden frame. Using the rawhide strip, he wove it crosswise through the holes. When finished and dried, he coated the snowshoes with beeswax to make them waterproof.

Anxious to try them out, Joseph strapped on his pair and Leah tried to strap on Nick's rather large ones. Standing on them, the little girl looked around, grinning. Nick told her that as soon as he had the time, he would make a smaller pair especially for her.

One evening, Miranda was quietly working on her biology course and Nick offered to help Joseph with his schoolwork. The boy said he hated schoolwork and didn't know why he should have to do any. He said that because he was Indian, he wouldn't have much chance to make anything out of his life, anyway. Taken aback, Nick only said something about sometimes having to do things whether we wanted to or not. The next day when he took Joseph snow shoeing and they sat down to rest on a large log, Nick used the opportunity to talk.

"Joseph, if you think just because you're Indian, you can't make anything of your life, then maybe you should know about an Indian by the name of Tommy Prince." Nick reached into his pocket and took out two chocolate bars, handing one to the boy.

"Thanks. Joseph quickly ripped the wrapper open. "Who's Tommy Prince?" he asked, taking a big bite.

"Tommy Prince just happens to be Canada's most decorated war hero."

"An Indian is the greatest war hero in all of Canada?" an incredulous Joseph replied. "How come I didn't learn about him in school?"

"Schools don't seem to teach much history anymore," Nick said, rising to his feet, tucking their empty chocolate bar wrappers in his pocket. "If you're interested, I'll tell you Tommy's story. But, maybe we should wait until after supper so your mom and Leah can hear it, too. How's that?"

"Sure," Joseph said, standing up. All of a sudden his right leg buckled and he teetered sideways. Arms flailing, the boy fell face first into the snow.

Covered with white powder, Joseph started to get up. He put one arm on the snow and pushed. His arm shot straight down, the snow to his armpit, his face buried again.

Nick howled with laughter. "I guess I forgot to tell you, but getting up on snowshoes is the hard part." He stepped over and extended his hand.

"Tommy Prince was born around 1915 on the Broken head Indian reserve in Manitoba." Nick began the story that night. "Although he was small for his age, of the eleven children in his family, Tommy was by far the most active. Growing up, whatever he lacked in stature, he more then made up for in energy and determination."

"Was he a full-blooded Indian or Métis?" Miranda was curious.

"Tommy was a direct descendant of a Chief of the Ojibwa tribe. From the time he was very young, his father spent many long days with him in the woods, teaching him all about hunting, tracking, and going through the bush so silently that even the animals couldn't detect him. These skills would become invaluable to Tommy in later years because when World War II broke out, he enlisted in the Royal Canadian Engineers."

"He was an engineer? I thought you said he was a soldier," Joseph asked.

"Sorry to confuse you, Joseph. The Royal Canadian Engineers are part of the Canadian army. Between 1939 and 1945 Canada was at war with Germany and Tommy volunteered to fight for his country. After basic training, he eventually signed up for the paratroopers. During his time in the military, Tommy demonstrated exceptional abilities with a rifle and was one of the best marksman, in the entire Canadian army."

"Wow," Joseph whispered the word, his eyes locked on Nick.

"I think Tommy was probably about as good with a rifle as that Indian boy from Carmacks is with a slingshot. What's his name?" Nick grinned, looking at Leah.

"My brother, Joseph!" Leah screamed in delight and Joseph beamed ear to ear.

"Well, with all the things he had learned in his boyhood, Tommy Prince was well suited for a very special kind of stealth combat. And so, out of more than one million Canadian soldiers, he was one of the few chosen to be part of an elite battalion. Now, this was a very select group of only the most skilled and brave soldiers who would be asked to take great risks behind enemy lines. The Canadian boys were merged with a similarly trained American army unit to form a battalion of uniquely skilled soldiers. I'm not sure of its exact official name, but because the

German soldiers soon came to fear them so much, they nicknamed them "The Devil's Brigade."

"Cool," Joseph said.

"As paratroopers, they were parachuted in behind enemy lines on missions to destroy strategic targets. This team soon gained fame for their skill in raiding and attacking the enemy objective, but what really set them apart was their ability to sneak up on the enemy at night. They could launch a devastating attack and then vanish before the enemy even knew what hit them. The Devil's Brigade commandoes were so skilled in stealth tactics that they once recaptured an entire town in France without ever firing a shot."

A wide-eyed Joseph absorbed every word but Nick noticed that although little Leah was too small to understand, her mother was equally as fascinated as her son.

Nick continued: "One time, while on a mission in Italy, Sergeant Prince's assignment was so dangerous that he chose to go alone rather than risk the lives of any of the men under his command. He made his way to an abandoned farmhouse where he crept to within a few hundred feet of the German front line. The only connection between him and his unit, who were firing their big cannons from nearly a mile away, was a thin telephone line leading across an open field. From his hiding place, Tommy could radio back to his unit and tell them exactly where the targets were located and where their shells were landing. However, during his watch, a mortar shell landed in the field and the explosion severed his communication line. Knowing how important his mission was, Tommy decided he had to do something about the broken communication line. Dressed in old coveralls and shirt that he got from a nearby farmhouse, Tommy picked up a garden hoe and went out into the field pretending to be the farmer weeding his crop. In full view of the enemy soldiers, as cool as could be, Tommy Prince slowly worked his way across the field to where the communication line had been severed. Bending down as though he were simply pulling weeds, he repaired the line. Casually, he then made his way back to the farmhouse where he continued his radio communications to his squad until they completely destroyed four key enemy positions."

"Boy, wait till I tell all the guys at my school," Joseph's voice held an edge of resolute pride.

"But there is much more to his story," Nick told him. "Shortly after the fighting ended, Sergeant Prince was summoned to Buckingham Palace in London where the King of England personally decorated him with the Canadian Military Medal and on behalf of the President of the United States, Tommy was awarded the American Silver Star for gallantry in action."

Miranda moved to organize things for the morning breakfast. "Tommy Prince showed that an Indian can be just as successful as any white man, don't you think, Joseph?" Miranda asked of her son.

"I guess," the young boy said, clearly impressed by the story.

"Ah, but his military career didn't end with the war in Europe," Nick said. "A few years later, Tommy Prince volunteered to join the Special Forces going to fight the war in Korea. That would have been around 1951 when he became part of a Canadian contingent with the United Nations troops fighting the communists. In Korea, Tommy was right in the middle of one of some of the toughest battles of the War."

"Do you think Tommy Prince was ever afraid?" Joseph wanted to know.

"I'm certain he was, it's perfectly normal to be afraid." Miranda said.

"Your mom is right, Joseph." Nick added. "Fear is actually a good thing. It's what prevents us from doing stupid things. Tommy Prince took great risks, but he knew he had certain skills and he believed in his abilities."

"Was Tommy Prince ever wounded—-or captured by the enemy?" Joseph asked.

"Wounded, yes. Captured, never. But, after all the tough battles for so many years during the wars, it took its toll on Tommy. His knees were damaged and he was sent home to a desk job. But, pushing pencils wasn't for Tommy Prince, no sir. Bad knees and all, he asked to return to active duty in Korea where he was once again in the middle of some of the worse fighting."

"Did we win the Korean war?" an innocent Joseph asked.

"Actually, nobody won. In mid 1953 an Armistice was signed, ending the fighting. Tommy Prince returned to Canada where he became active in Indian affairs. When he died, over five hundred people attended his funeral, including military delegations from both Canada and the United States plus the governments of France, Italy and Britain sent representatives to honor a great soldier who had fought for their freedom."

Nick rose to get a drink of water. "Now, Joseph. If you think just because you're Indian that you can't make anything of your life, you had better think again. I hope that by me telling you a little about Tommy Prince it will help you believe in yourself. Tommy proved that we all have the potential to do great things. Where you come from, or the color of your skin, has nothing to do with your abilities. It's what's inside, and how you use it, that really counts."

"When I grow up, I want to join the army and be just like Tommy Prince," Joseph said, filled with enthusiasm.

Nick told him a military career was a worthy occupation but that he didn't have to join the army to fight battles because there were many more battles to be fought right here at home with poverty, alcoholism, and other social problems. "There is always a greater need for people helping one another, than fighting," he said.

Joseph was too young to fully comprehend what Nick was trying to say but he wanted to learn more. "How many medals did Tommy Prince get?"

"Ten or eleven while he was alive, and I think at least two more after his death."

Miranda looked at her watch. "Bed time, big guy."

While she tucked Joseph into bed, Nick placed a pot of water on the stove for tea. When they sat down, she challenged him to a game of cribbage. After Miranda had won three games in a row, he was still not about to give up. Determined, he took her on one more time, got beat again, and with a good-natured grumble, said it was time for bed.

Lying in the darkness, their wilderness silence was broken only by the faint howl of a night wind in the trees and the occasional crackle from the heater in the middle of the tepee. At least once during the night, Nick got up and added wood to the stove but even so, by morning the fire would usually be little more than glowing ashes.

As was his ritual, Nick rose early, filled the heater with wood, and put the tea on. By the time tea was ready, it would be warm in the tepee. On this morning, he had just started breakfast when Joseph, sitting up in his bed, asked: "Can we go hunting today, Nick?"

Nick thought for a minute before answering. "We can if the wind dies down."

Not wanting to be left out, Leah hollered, "Can I go hunting with you?"

"Not today, Leah. The snow is too deep and we only have two pairs of snowshoes."

"You promised to make me a pair, remember?" she reminded him.

"You are right, I did promise. How about if Joseph and I go hunting today and we bring back the wood to make you and your mom snowshoes. Then, I'll take you hunting."

Leah seemed satisfied with that and by the time they finished breakfast, the wind had died down enough so that Nick and Joseph began preparing for their hunting trip.

CHAPTER 10

The Hunting Trip

NICK AND JOSEPH dressed in their warmest clothing, put on their newly made snowshoes, and headed west towards the open prairie. Just before getting there, they turned north and walked along the edge of the bush, so they would be travelling downwind from any game.

The wind had drifted the snow just enough to form a light crust, making it easy walking on snowshoes. The prairie ahead of them was about a mile wide and three miles long, with low hills on both sides and the St. Elias mountain range to the north. The low hills made easy escaping from predators for deer and moose that liked to graze early in the morning on the valley grasses that were exposed by the wind.

After walking for more than an hour, they noticed a large flock of ptarmigan, feeding on buds in clumps of low bushes that were spread across the valley. Nick kicked off his snowshoes and got down on his belly as low as he could. Joseph followed his every move as they crawled to within thirty feet of the birds without being seen.

They buried down in the snow with only the tops of their heads showing. Joseph fired his slingshot and missed with the first shot, but his second shot found its target. A ptarmigan lay still on the surface of the snow. Nick told him to keep shooting. He shot three more times, before he hit another one. Then, they both started shooting. The ptarmigan were in a feeding frenzy and didn't even notice them. When it was all over, they gathered up seven ptarmigan, enough for two good meals. They cleaned them and laid the remains out on the snow for the fox, mink, and weasels to feed on.

They continued north along the edge of the bush for another hour, when they noticed some dark shadows moving amidst the tall spruce trees. As they moved in a little closer, they counted

Charging moose.

eleven moose, that were yarded up on the side of a hill. They decided to cut down some of the taller willows so that the younger moose could browse on the tender buds. After moving in a little too close to the herd, Nick looked up and saw a large bull with only one antler charging directly towards them. With one swipe of the trusty axe, he cut down a seven-foot pine tree and it over his head he ran towards the bull yelling and waving his hands. He was relieved when the bull moose stopped within twenty feet of them, turned around and ran back to the herd.

Joseph's eyes were wide as saucers when he asked, "Why did you do that? How did you know the moose would turn and run?"

"I didn't. I just took a chance. If I could make myself look big enough, I could bluff him out. I was lucky this time I guess. Don't you ever try that. There's only about one chance in ten the moose will turn and run away and that was it. Did you notice that the bull had lost one of its antlers? That's probably why he decided not to fight. This time of the year they lose their antlers and will grow them back in the spring. Anyway, we better get out of here before he realizes it was only a pine tree over my head that made me look so big."

It was dark when they got back to camp. Leah was standing by the table with a big smile on her face, holding up two reed door-mats.

"Look what we made today," she said. "Mom and I went down by the river and picked some bull rushes to make these mats so you can wipe the snow off your feet. Do you like them?"

Nick looked at them and said, "That's some pretty nice work you girls did. They're just what we need. Look what we got in this bag. Seven ptarmigan." He showed her the contents of the bag.

"Joseph is getting to be a pretty good hunter. He shot most of them himself," Nick remarked proudly.

The birds Joseph had cleaned and cut up on the prairie were divided into two packages. They would freeze one to be used later. The second package would be used that night to make a big pot of ptarmigan stew.

Everyone helped making dinner, and later with the dishwashing. Joseph told the girls all about being charged by the bull moose and how Nick held a pine tree over his head and ran towards the moose yelling and waving the tree at it.

"Weren't you afraid?" Leah asked.

"Sure I was, but not as frightened as that big bull moose when he saw me come running through the bush with that tree over my head. I must have looked pretty scary to make him turn around and run."

"Nick? Would you tell us a story as soon as we get into bed?" Leah asked.

"Not tonight, Leah. I think we've heard enough stories. Let's all go to bed early ,get some sleep and I'll tell you a story tomor-row night," he answered tiredly.

Nick had been sleeping for only minutes when he heard Miranda calling, "Nick... Nicholas! I think I hear somebody out-side calling."

Nick listened for a while. It was deathly quiet out there, not even a breath of wind to move branches of the trees. Even the stove in the center of the tepee wasn't making any crackling noise.

"Maybe it's a wolf you heard. They sound almost human sometimes. I can't hear anything," Nick said as he drifted off back to sleep.

Miranda lay there for a long time listening, with her eyes wide open, staring at the ceiling of the teepee. Again, she heard the sound outside. It was much clearer this time. She was positive someone was out there needing help.

"Nick....Nick," she whispered, trying not to wake up the children. "That sound, it's out there. I heard it again."

"The closest village is Aishihik, on Sekulmun Lake, twenty miles south of here. I don't think you could hear anybody calling from that distance, no matter how loud they hollered. I'll go outside and listen for a while and see if I can hear anything," Nick reassured her.

He got dressed, put a kettle of water on the heater for tea, and went outside to listen.

It was a cold, clear winter night. The moon was full and the northern lights danced in the sky. The bands of brilliant blue and scarlet light shimmered and shifted to and fro. He listened for twenty minutes and couldn't hear a thing. Finally, he got too cold and went back inside.

The water on the stove was boiling. He brewed a pot of tea, poured two cups, and handed one to Miranda, as he sat down on the edge of her bed. He had a concerned look on his face as he told her, "Maybe you've been out here in the bush a little too long. Maybe you're hearing things that aren't really there. Sometimes that happens to people."

"No! I'm not going crazy. I know what I heard. I know there's someone out there," she insisted.

"I didn't say you were crazy. I just said that sometimes when people are isolated for a long period of time, they start to hear things that aren't really there," he replied.

Nick sat on Miranda's bed, just listening for a long time. Then he said, "I may as well go back to bed. I can't hear anything."

Moving over to give Nick some room, Miranda asked, "Would

you please lay down here beside be for a while and keep me company? I can't sleep anyway."

When Nick lay down beside her, she put her hand on the side of his head and rubbing his ear she said. "Nick, you're a wonderful man. You've got a heart of gold. You've been so good to the children and me."

"We're all good to one another, even the kids are getting along better, sharing things and helping each other," Nick said in a whisper.

Miranda moved her hand behind Nick's neck and slowly pulled him towards her. Their lips touched for a moment and parted. When they touched again, Nick moved his hand behind Miranda's back and pulled her body tightly against his. The other hand moved behind her head as they kissed tenderly.

Suddenly, their heads pulled back. Their eyes were wide open as they lay there motionless, staring at each other. They both heard it. It was a human voice. Someone was out there calling for help.

"I heard it clearly that time. Whoever is out there is in trouble. I have to go and see if I can find them," Nick said as he jumped up from the bed.

"Nick, do you realize it's eleven o'clock at night and forty below zero outside," Miranda reminded him.

"I know, and that's all the more reason I have to go right now. Whoever is out there won't last the night. They'll freeze to death. I hope I can find them before it's too late."

Nick poured the last of the tea in a thermos, dressed himself as warm as he could, grabbed a sleeping bag, and headed south in the direction the sound was coming from.

The light from the moon, the stars, and northern lights reflecting off the snow made it almost as bright as daylight. The only sound was the crunching of his snowshoes as he picked his way through the trees. He kept up an almost trotting pace for over twenty minutes before he stopped to listen. Then he called and listened again. There was complete silence, not a whisper. He continued south, in the direction of Aishihik, for another twenty minutes. Again, he stopped and hollered, "Hello, hello out there."

Then, from a willow bluff a hundred yards straight ahead of him, came a faint, chilling voice, that made him quiver.

"Help! Help me."

He found himself running as fast as he could towards the bluff. As he entered it, he could make out an outline of someone lying face down in the snow. When he lifted the man's head, he was astonished when he recognized it was his friend Jerry, half buried in snow.

Nick used one of his snowshoes to shovel the snow away from around Jerry's body. Gently turning him over onto his back, he saw that his foot was caught in a bear trap. No doubt it was one the poachers had set and left the previous summer.

"It's my leg. I think it's broken," Jerry whimpered.

"Don't try talking now. Just lie back and relax while I get your leg out of this trap."

Nick placed his feet on the springs on either side of the trap, and with his half frozen hands, pulled the steel jaws apart. At the same time, he used his teeth to clench onto Jerry's pant leg and by moving his head backwards, lifted the leg out of the trap. Nick then removed his scarf, tore it in half, and bandaged up the bleeding leg, as best he could. He then covered Jerry with the sleeping bag and lit a roaring fire beside him.

When the fire became hot enough, Nick cut two poles to prop open the sleeping bag to let in as much heat as possible. He knew he had to warm up Jerry's body before moving him any distance in that cold weather.

After an hour went by, he zipped Jerry up inside the sleeping bag, put out the fire, and put on the snowshoes.

Lifting Jerry onto his shoulders was no easy task, but he finally managed to get him on and balanced. The extra weight made it tough going, even on snowshoes. The limp body on his shoulder grew heavier and heavier with every step. He had to stop and rest every two or three hundred yards. Sometimes, he would sit down and roll Jerry off into the snow beside him, or sometimes just lean up against a tree for a few minutes.

It was bright enough out to make it easy for follow his tracks back to the camp.

Finally, he saw the tepee in the distance. The light burning inside made it appear like a huge Japanese lantern nestled amongst the trees, with a plume of blue smoke funnelling upward towards the sky. The air outside was so cold he had wrapped what was left of his scarf around his nose and mouth to keep the cold air from freezing his lungs.

It was three o'clock in the morning by the time he got Jerry back to camp. Miranda had anticipated Nick would be bringing someone back with him, so she cleared an area at the foot of Nick's bed and heated some rocks on the stove. As soon as they got Jerry inside the tepee and onto the bed, they removed all his clothing except for his long, grey woollen underwear, which they cut off at the knee. His leg was badly cut and there were chunks of skin hanging loose on both sides, but he was lucky not to have any broken bones.

They placed the hot rocks all around his body to warm him up. Miranda then cleaned and bandaged the wound. All the while, Jerry was mumbling something about his children coming to visit him. He was in shock and they knew that once they stopped the bleeding and got him warmed up, he would probably be okay. The tips of his fingers were white from frostbite, as were his toes and his left ear.

Miranda sat beside him rubbing his fingers and side of his neck, while Nick brewed a fresh pot of coffee, then started Massaging his toes. They knew this was going to be a long night.

It was ten o'clock in the morning before Jerry opened his eyes. "How did you find me? How did I get here?" Jerry asked. "I remember stepping on the bear trap and trying for hours to get my foot free. I also remember lying in the snow hollering for help as loud as I could, but I didn't think anyone would ever hear me."

"You're lucky there wasn't any wind out there last night and that Miranda wouldn't listen to me when I told her she was hearing things. She was very persistent in what she heard and didn't give up until she had me convinced."

Jerry's ankle was swollen and sore, but he was glad to be alive. He couldn't put any weight on his leg, so Nick and Joseph cut a couple of willows and made him a set of crutches.

The crutches were fine for getting around inside the tepee, but when he tried them outside in the snow, he fell flat on his face. They laughed as Joseph helped him up and brushed off the snow. Nick constructed a chair out of sticks and an old blanket where Jerry could sit outside and watch everyone else cut and split wood.

That afternoon, while the fire was burning outside, they heated the rocks for the sweat lodge. When it was hot enough, Miranda and Leah went in first. Nick, Jerry, and Joseph went in after they were finished. It was a tight squeeze, but once they were in, Jerry tried teaching them an Indian song he learned when he was a young boy. It was about an old Indian hunter dying and going to the big hunting grounds in the sky. Nick and Joseph had a hard time pronouncing some of the words, and Jerry had a hard time trying to remember all the verses.

When they went back into the tepee from the sweat lodge, Miranda redid the bandage on Jerry's ankle.

That night, Jerry told the kids a story about a raven that couldn't fly, but before the story was finished, they had both fallen asleep. Jerry looked at them and said, "I guess they didn't like my story very much. They couldn't even stay awake for the ending."

"That's good," Nick said. "Now you can tell them the rest of the story tomorrow night."

"Tomorrow night?" Jerry said. "How long do you think I'm going to spend here?"

"Well, I'd say probably another week or so before you're ready to make the twenty-mile trip, back to your cabin at Sekulmun Lake. I don't want to have to find you in the bush again and have to carry you back here. Once in a lifetime is enough for me," Nick explained.

The weather stayed clear and cold for the next week. It would get to minus thirty-five or forty at night and warm up to minus eight or ten in the daytime, which was mild for that time of the year in the Yukon.

Jerry's leg was getting a little better every day.

He used his spare time to make Leah a small pair of snowshoes. She was so happy, she put them on and walked around and around the tepee.

Mid-week, Jerry went along on some short trips into the woods. He had been trapping with his father since he was five years old and was an expert on wild animals and their behaviours. They all learned a lot from him, and he was always joking with them. Sometimes they didn't know whether to believe him or not, but he would always set them straight in the end.

By the end of the week, Jerry's leg was well enough for him to travel. They were preparing to leave in the morning. The weather was holding steady with some light winds. They decided they would all go along as far as where he got caught in the bear trap. Nick had hung Jerry's packsack high in a tree and had to show him where to find it.

Daylight was just breaking as they started retracing their tracks to the bluff. Leah started off walking on her new snowshoes, but after half a mile couldn't keep up and ended up on Nick's back.

It was noon when they found the bluff where Jerry's packsack was hanging. They lit a fire and toasted their sandwiches before splitting up and each heading home.

CHAPTER 11

The Wolverine

ONE NIGHT NICK WOKE UP to hear a ruffling sound just outside the tepee. It was quite cold inside; the fire had almost gone out. He filled the heater with wood and listened in the darkness. Again he could hear a scratching sound outside. An animal of some kind was out there. He would have to go out and investigate. Their whole winters supply of meat was out there. It meant the difference between survival or starvation.

Nick dressed, picked up a flashlight, and went outside. He headed straight towards the ground cache where all the meat was stored. He saw where something had been digging under the logs that were placed over the cache. His worst fear came upon him. He knew only a wolverine would be smart enough to do something like that.

A wolverine is an animal about the size of a large dog, with shiny, almost black fur. Two yellowish strips start just behind its shoulders and run along either side of its back, joining at its rump. It has a round head with a short snout, white teeth, and long white claws. It is very cunning. Pound for pound, it's the most ferocious and gluttonous animals on the face of this earth. They've been known to tackle a grizzly bear and come out a winner. Indians have said that the wolverine is part bear, part skunk, and the rest pure devil. They called it "Car cay" an Indian word meaning "devil."

When Nick removed a few of the logs, he saw where the wolverine had come to within a foot of the

Wolverine.

three hundred pounds of meat that was stored under there. He knew the wolverine would be back later that night. All the meat would have to be moved up into the high cache before then. It was cold enough outside that the meat would stay frozen up there.

Nick had just started carrying the meat up to the high cache when he heard something coming towards him. It seemed too big to be the wolverine. He climbed all the way onto the high cache and was about to pull the ladder up behind him, when he heard Miranda's voice say.

"What the heck are you doing out here in the middle of the night?"

"Miranda. You scared the daylights out of me. There's a wolverine out here trying to steal the meat out of our ground cache. I have to move it all up here tonight."

"Okay, you stay there, and I'll pass the meat up to you."

It was six o'clock in morning by the time they had all the meat moved up to the high cache. The northern lights lit up the sky; it was a cold, clear, night. It would be another four hours before daylight.

When they returned to the tepee, it was piping hot inside. Miranda forgot to turn down the heater after filling it with wood.

High cache.

They were too excited to go back to sleep. Miranda put the coffee on and started studying her biology course. Nick decided to cut about two dozen strips from the dry cedar log and start making arrows.

For arrowheads, he used chips of shale that he had gathered in the fall. He cut slits in the cedar shafts, slid in the heads, and bound them together with rawhide that had been soaking overnight in water. To make the arrows fly straight and true, he used the tail feathers he had saved from the ptarmigans. By the time he finished his second arrow, Joseph was up and dressed.

"Nick, you promised you would let me help make the arrows."

"Joseph, what are you doing up so early? Why don't you sleep for a little while longer?"

"I don't want to sleep. I want to help you make the arrows!"

"Okay. You cut the slots in the shafts, and I'll shape the heads."

When they had all the heads bound onto the shafts, they cut the ptarmigan feathers, then glued and bound them to the shafts with thread. Next, they cut grooves in the end to fit the rawhide string on the bow.

As soon as they were finished making the arrows, Joseph wanted to go hunting. Nick told him they couldn't go hunting that day because the night before a wolverine almost got into their ground cache and stole their meat supply. They would have to make the high cache more secure.

After breakfast, they went outside and trampled down the snow under the high cache. They poured water on the posts that held up the cache. This created ice around the posts to make it harder for the wolverine to climb. Next, they cut willows about two feet long, sharpening them on one end, and tied them around the posts with the points facing downward. After spending all day out there, Nick felt that their meat supply would now be secure.

The next night, Miranda came over to Nick's bed, nudged him and told him that she could hear something scratching outside. Nick listened for a while.

"It's that wolverine. He's out there again." He hurriedly put on his clothes and ran outside. In the moonlight he could see an outline of the wolverine on the platform of the high cache.

When the wolverine saw Nick coming towards him, it jumped

the fifteen feet from the platform to the ground and ran into the bushes.

Nick noticed a tall poplar tree beside the high cache that the wolverine must have climbed. When it neared the top, the limb bent far enough over and the wolverine just dropped down onto the platform.

Nick took his axe and chopped down the poplar tree, hoping it would prevent the wolverine from reaching the cache.

Less than twenty minutes later, the noise was back. There was no doubt what it was. Nick dressed again, went outside and saw that the wolverine had chewed off some of the sharpened willows that were tied around the tree. He knew the wolverine would never give up. He put the ladder up to the high cache, brought down a five-pound moose roast and put it on a stump where the wolverine could find it. Then, he took the ladder down and went back into the tepee.

In the morning the meat was gone. There was only one thing on Nick's mind: survival. The wolverine would have to be destroyed. It was a matter of the animal or themselves.

The question was how to get rid of such a cunning menace with as little pain and suffering as possible. Nick thought it would be best to build a deadfall trap.

He cleared away the snow and drove stakes into the frozen ground in a two-foot semicircle. Then, he placed two ten-inch logs across the opening and drove in two poles on either side so the logs could slide up and down. He then laid two twelve-foot logs lengthwise over the top of the first logs. He propped the top log up

Dead fall trap.

with two sticks, which he tied to the bait hanging in the middle of the trap. When the wolverine pulled on the bait, the logs would come down, crushing his skull.

That night when everyone else was asleep, Nick lay awake listening for any sound outside that would indicate the wolverine was caught in the trap. Finally, he drifted off to sleep; he didn't know how long it was before he was awakened by a loud bang. The trap had been sprung, and then there was only silence. There was no sound of a struggle. The wolverine probably didn't even know what hit it.

Nick got up early in the morning and went out to confirm his kill. When he got to the trap, the logs were down, the bait was gone, but there was no wolverine in the trap. The wolverine had put its head into the trap, grabbed the bait, and pulled its head out before the logs came crushing down. The wolverine had the moose meat, and Nick still had the problem.

He would have to change the design of the trap. Instead of pulling the bait to release the logs, he put it in the back of the trap and rigged it so the logs would fall as soon as the wolverine reached inside to get it.

The next morning when Nick went out to check the trap, he saw where the wolverine had tried to dig under the stakes to get to the meat. It was reluctant to put its head in the trap a second time. Nick cut up the bait in small bits this time and placed them about six inches apart from the mouth of the trap, through to the back.

The following morning the logs were down and the wolverine lay motionless in the trap. Nick took the wolverine out of the trap, skinned it and cut the meat up into pieces. He kept only the meat from the hind legs and part of the tender meat from along the back. The rest he scattered in the bush a mile away, so as not to attract any animals to the camp. It would take him two weeks to finish tanning the hide.

CHAPTER 12

Falling Through the Ice

WAKENED BY THE PIERCING COLD inside the tepee, Nick shuddered as he hurried to dress. He had slept through the night and the fire had all but gone out. Outside, the morning temperature hovered around fifty below zero; inside the tepee, it didn't feel much warmer. He put dry kindling in the heater and when he blew on the ashes, the flames burst forth immediately. As soon as the kindling was burning strong, he filled the stove with dry wood then grabbed a pail and headed down to the river to get water.

During the night, new snow had fallen and the winds swept high drifts, filling the path to the stream. In the waist-high snow, he slugged his way through, his mind still dwelling on his failure to take care of the fire. Their food would be frozen as would anything liquid they had, even if it had been stored in a case. Miranda had entrusted him with the safety of her and her children and subjecting them to any form of carelessness was unacceptable.

With his mind still occupied he was not as alert as he should have been and he had taken only a few steps out onto the river's frozen edge when he heard a crack then all at once felt his body falling. Freezing-cold water shocked his system and a numbing fear gripped him as the snow caved in around him.

Surfacing in the frigid waters, he had to fight from being pulled under by the rapid swirling stream. Against the current, he gripped the icy ledge, trying to gather his thoughts. When his feet suddenly touched the bottom, a great sigh of relief came, and he stood up. Although the water was only up to his chest, his relieved mindset changed instantly back to anxiety when his effort to climb out proved futile. Struggling, the current kept knocking his feet out from under him. Several times he tried to get a grip and lift him self out of the water. The feeling in his arms and legs was dis-

Falling through the ice.

appearing and he knew survival depended on his ability to get out of the icy water within the next minute or two at the most.

Pulling as much snow as he could into the hole around him, in sheer desperation he bent his knees, squatting down underwater and lunged up grabbing a small tree branch sticking out from a snow-covered log. Able to wiggle up enough to inch his way across the ice, he kept tugging the branch and pulled himself up the icy riverbank. Finally, he made it to his feet and started walking back towards the tepee. Grateful that it was only a short distance away, the sense of relief he had felt before came back only to abruptly change one more time when his clothing froze solid and he could no longer stand upright. On his hands and knees, he began crawling back to the tepee but the snow was so deep it was impossible for him to make any headway. He hollered as loud as he could. "Miranda—-Help! Help me!"

Concerned by the length of time Nick had been gone, Miranda checked outside. His footprints led from the door of the tepee towards the stream. She checked around the tepee to see that the water bucket was missing from its usual spot on the shelf.

Knowing he should have covered the short distance to the stream and back in a matter of minutes, an alarmed Miranda dressed to go look for him.

With Joseph on her heels, Miranda followed the tracks leading down to the stream. All at once he was there, lying in the snow in front of her. Together, Miranda and Joseph tugged on Nick's jacket as hard as they could but were barley able to move him an inch. Desperate, a panic-stricken Miranda told Joseph to stay with him while she went and brought back the horse.

Exhausted by the time she got to the corral, she struggled to open the gate against the heavy snow. She removed the halter from where Nick had hooked it on a tree, and led the horse down the path as fast as she could. With Joseph's help, she tied one end of the rope under Nick's arms and the other around the horse's chest. Urging the horse forward, Nick's limp body slid across the snow to the door of the tepee. A frightened Leah held the door open while Joseph and Miranda strained to pull him inside.

Miranda quickly cut off his frozen clothing, wrapped him in warm blankets, and opened the damper on the heater to make the tepee as warm as possible. For more than an hour, an anxious Miranda sat next to him, watching for any sign that he was coming to. When Nick opened his eyes, he gave her only a blank look, then closed them again.

When he came to the second time, she propped his back up against thick cushions, and fed him hot broth. The children sat on the foot of the bed, watching without saying a word until the last of the soup was gone. Then, Leah moved to stand next to Nick, wrapped her arms around his neck, and squeezed her cheek against his. An uncertain and fearful Joseph tried to put up a brave front. With a sad smile he said. "Nick, you'll be okay, I promise. And, I'll keep the heater full of wood so you'll be nice and warm."

Even with the warm broth, Nick shivered with deep chills until suddenly his whole body began to sweat. At first, Miranda used a towel to wipe his forehead and chest but soon had to change his drenched bed sheets. With only one extra set of sheets she had to rinse them in the washtub and hang them across the top of the tepee to dry. By four-thirty in the afternoon, when the heavy sweating subsided, she had had to wash and dry his sheets six times.

He remained in a coma for the next two days. Leah stayed in the tepee with him, while Joseph and Miranda went out gathering firewood. They kept the tepee hot inside and Nick as warm as possible. On the second evening Leah leaned over, looking at him with tears in her eyes and said, "Nick, please don't die. We all love you. We need you very much."

"Don't worry Leah, Nick is a strong man. He'll come back to us soon," Miranda reassured her daughter, doubting her own words.

In the afternoon of the third day, Nick finally opened his eyes. Leah was there, and at the sight of him awake, a wide smile came followed by tears of joy. "Nick, you're alive!" the child screamed.

When Miranda and Joseph returned with a load of wood, Leah blurted out, "Mom! Look! Nick's awake!"

The armload of wood spilled onto the floor as Miranda raced to his bedside. The anxiety she felt, clearly visible on her face, turned to a warm smile as she reached to take his hand.

"How long have I been asleep?" Nick looked at her, his voice barely above a whisper.

"More than two days." She told him. "Now don't try talking anymore until I can get some hot food into you. Are you hungry?"

"I could eat a horse," he said.

"We still need the horse, how about some moose meat?"

It was almost Christmas by the time Nick fully recovered from his bout with pneumonia. So much time spent in bed brought was filled with assessing his carelessness. His letting the fire go out on a bitterly cold night was minor compared to his failure to pay attention to the dangers of thin ice under deceptively heavy snow.

This land could be very unforgiving; if you made the slightest mistake, it would make you pay dearly.

CHAPTER 13

Christmas in the Tepee

THE WEEK BEFORE CHRISTMAS, they decorated the inside of the tepee with spruce boughs and put up a small tree. Outside, with logs and a few bales of hay, they built a manger at the side of the tent.

For a long time, Nick had been wondering what he could make for the children that would surprise them. For Miranda, he already had the jeans and sweater he had purchased on his trip to Whitehorse. Christmas was the perfect occasion to give them to her. He would give Joseph the new hunting knife and sheath he had brought for himself from Vancouver, but for Leah, he had nothing. He had no idea what she would like but she seemed easy to please and content with whatever she had. For her, he wanted a surprise, something that would really make her excited.

Just four days before Christmas, he snow shoed up the mountain to get cedar root for making Christmas baskets. While digging under the snow he caught sight of a pack of wolves gathered around a fresh kill on the side of the far slope. Curious, he began hiking across the ridge to get a closer look. On the way, the distinct baaing of a lamb drew his attention to a clump of small spruce trees. Standing on four shaky legs, the cries of the frightened baby lamb grew louder as he approached.

Nick felt certain the wolves had just killed its mother. She had used herself to distract the wolf pack, ultimately giving up her life to save her baby. The lamb was much too young for that time of year and must have been born late in the season. The tragedy was that it had little chance for survival even with its mother alive. Now though, the lamb would not last out the day.

Nick picked it up, put it inside his jacket, and took it back to camp. Once there, he moved as quickly as possible, hoping the lamb would stay quiet. He took it to the smokehouse thinking that if he could hide it for a few days, the lamb would make a perfect Christmas gift for Leah.

He arranged several bales of hay in the corner of the smokehouse to make a warm bed. But, more than anything, the lamb needed nourishment right away. Nick went to the tepee, and, disguising his actions from the others, mixed some powered milk in a pail and brought it out to the lamb. He placed two fingers inside the lamb's mouth and guided its head down to the milk. The lamb drank all the milk in just a few minutes. It would have to be fed every four hours for the next couple of days.

Before long, the lamb regained its strength and was bounding back and forth inside the smokehouse. Fortunately, it stayed quiet, and Leah was none the wiser about her Christmas gift. Whenever Nick got up in the middle of the night to put wood in the stove, he would sneak warm milk out to the smokehouse and feed the little lamb. From the hay scattered on the floor, he knew it had begun eating hay between feedings, which meant he could soon extend its feedings to every eight hours.

On Christmas morning, Joseph and Leah were up early. He had already lit the candles on the little Christmas tree, and the children were anxious to open their presents. Miranda told them they had to eat breakfast first but she rushed everything, just as anxious as the kids to open the gifts. Soon, a beaming Miranda began passing out the presents.

She had made pairs of mittens for both Leah and Joseph. For Nick, she had made a pair of mitts that came up to his elbows and had wolverine fur around the tops. Nick was very surprised she had managed to do all that work right under his eyes without him ever noticing. Too, he was thrilled at how beautiful they were and thanked her profusely for her thoughtfulness.

Miranda was pleased and excited when she opened her presents and saw the new sweater and jeans. Joseph had a proud look on his face when he strapped on the leather sheath with the shiny new hunting knife buckled inside.

When all the presents were opened, Nick said he would have a look outside to see if there was anything else they had forgotten. He put his hat and parka on and went to the smokehouse. He took the lamb and placed it in the manger. Then he called, "Leah! Look out here. See what I found? I think it's for you."

Leah peered out the flap of the tepee and when she saw the little lamb in the manger, let out a scream. "Mom, look! It's...it's...a baby lamb," she ran outside with only her pajamas on. Nick told her to hurry and bring the lamb inside before she froze.

More than anyone else, Miranda was surprised by the lamb. "Nick, when and where did you get it?"

"The other day when I hiked into the mountains to get cedar root, I found it in the snow. The wolves had killed its mother so I had the choice between leaving it to die or bring it here." Nick looked at the lamb, hugged tight in Leah's arms. "Just look at that face. How could I leave something like that out in the mountains to die?"

Miranda smiled, looking over at the smokehouse. "I guess you kept it hidden in the smokehouse for the past few days."

"Yeah, and with all those late-night feedings, I've gotten attached to the darn thing!"

"Can we keep it inside the tepee with us, please, please?" Leah tugged at her mother's arm.

"Sure," Miranda told her. "It can sleep between you and Joseph."

"This is the best present I ever got in my whole life," Leah said.

Leah brought in some hay and made a bed for the lamb next to her own.

Before Leah got too attached to the lamb, and that was easy to do, Nick felt it best to explain to the little girl that her little fluffy lamb was a wild animal and always would be. "We can raise it until it is strong enough to survive on its own, but one day it will have to go back to its home in the wild."

Leah had many questions but she understood that a lamb born in the wild belonged in nature, not in their tepee. For the next couple of days, the lamb was the center of attention.

Leah and the lamb.

94

The daytime weather during Christmas week warmed up and Nick and Miranda took advantage of the opportunity to cut and haul firewood. Once the weather turned and it started to snow, strong winds came and the temperature dropped to forty below.

With almost zero visibility outside, for the next eight days they remained inside the tepee, entertaining themselves by telling stories, reading, and playing checkers. Story telling took on a ritual, one of them would make up a few lines and then the next one would take a turn, adding to the story. Most days, Miranda would spend time on her biology course and Nick would help Joseph with his schoolwork.

On the ninth day, of what by then they jokingly were calling their "incarceration," the weather broke. The winds died down and the sun came out. Although still quite cold, everyone was glad they were able to get out of the tepee. Even the little lamb seemed to enjoy bounding around in the snow, chasing after Leah, following her everywhere.

CHAPTER 14

Making Moccasins

NICK WAS PUTTING HIS BOOTS ON to go outside when he noticed one of them had a rip in it. Concerned, because he knew the boot wouldn't last the winter, he figured he would have to at least attempt to make a replacement pair. He remembered how he'd spent hours as a child watching a neighbor's wife make moccasins but that was a long time ago and he wasn't sure. However, given the circumstances, he had to try.

He retrieved the rest of the moose hide from its hook in the smokehouse. He cut out his foot pattern and allowed an extra inch around the edges for stitching. There was enough hide to make a pair of knee-length moccasins. He spent all day stitching them together and sewing decorative beads on the tops and along the sides. They didn't look quite like the ones from his childhood, but they were sturdy and would serve the purpose. When finished, he rubbed them with fish oil to make them waterproof and hung them beside the heater to dry.

When Nick went in the woods early the next morning to cut a supply of deadwood for the fire, a freezing wind whipped up the snow. Holding his head down from the blinding wind he could barely see as he cut, split, and stacked wood. He would have to wait for better weather before bringing out the horse to haul the wood back to the camp. By the time he returned to the tepee in the late afternoon, he was so tired he didn't even notice his new moccasins were no longer hanging by the heater.

He left early again the next morning and worked in the woods all day. It was dark by the time he got home. Miranda had dinner ready. Joseph, Leah, and the lamb greeted him, the little girl holding out her arms for hugs, ready to climb all over him.

Only when things quieted down a bit did Nick notice the moccasins. They were about the same size as the ones he had made, but there was something very different about them. The stitching was neat and even, and the beads sewn on the tops and sides were a work of art. He sat there, staring at them in disbelief, then asked: "Miranda? You made these?"

"They're the ones you made. I only fixed them up a bit."

"Where did you learn to make moccasins?"

"From watching you, I only improved on the technique."

By the time March rolled around, the days were getting noticeably longer and the weather was improving. Leah's little lamb began spending most of the day out-side, following Leah around like a puppy. Since Christmas, it had

Miranda making moccasins.

grown like a weed and Nick sat the little girl down to talk, reminding her again that soon they would have to take it back to the wild.

"How come we can't keep it with us all the time?" Leah asked even though she knew the answer.

"Because it was born to be wild, and it wouldn't be fair to keep it from living free with the other mountain sheep. When it grows up, it will have a family of its own. Now do you want to keep it from that?" Nick asked.

"No, I guess I don't. When do we have to take it back?" Leah asked, a resigned sadness in her voice.

"It's your lamb. You've been looking after it all winter. I think it's only fair that you decide when its time."

For the next few days Leah played with the lamb constantly, often cupping her hands over its ear, whispering. It was as if she was trying to explain why she had to take it back to the wild.

On the third day, she came up to Nick and calmly said. "My little lamb is ready to return to its own family now. Can I come with you when you take it back?"

"We can all go tomorrow, if the weather's good," Nick looked at her, a twinge of guilt taking hold at the sight of the child's melancholy face.

The sun was shining bright by eight o'clock the next morning. With their lunch packed, they were on their way up the mountain to try to find a flock of sheep that would be a family for the little lamb.

Nick, Miranda, and Joseph walked on snowshoes, with Leah sitting high on Nick's shoulders. Behind them, the lamb followed, trying to keep pace but frequently sinking a thin leg deep into the snow.

When they crossed the prairie and started up the mountain, the snow turned soft and mushy, making it slow going. By noon, they hadn't seen any signs of sheep and decided to head back home. It was well after dark by the time they got back to the tepee. Everyone was tired and went to bed soon after dinner. They wanted to get an early start in the morning.

The next day, they hiked farther along the prairie before starting up the mountain. There were a few signs where sheep had been digging for grass under the snow, but they were too old to be worth following. Once again, after a long day's walk, they had to return home with the lamb.

It was still dark outside when they left the tepee early on the third morning. They were half way across the prairie by the time the sun peeked over the mountain. They picked up a sheep trail and followed it for an hour before catching sight of a small herd lying down on the side of the mountain. If they could just get a little closer and let the lamb see the other sheep, it might just follow them.

A hard wind blew across the prairie and up the mountainside. Nick explained to the children the importance of being downwind so that the sheep's sensitive nose couldn't smell their scent and flee from the perceived danger. It took them over an hour to make their way behind a large boulder in a spot about three hundred yards above where the sheep were lying. Nick told Leah to quietly take the lamb towards the sheep and try to get it to go to them.

Leah walked slowly out from behind the boulder towards the

sheep with the little lamb following her. Several times she turned to look back at Nick until he motioned her to stop. The little girl moved behind the lamb and gave it a little push. To her surprise, the lamb started walking towards the other sheep. Leah turned and started running back. She was almost to the boulder when she turned to see the little lamb right on her heels.

Tears came as she started walking the lamb back towards the flock of sheep. When she was about halfway, she could see that some of the sheep were starting to stand up. The little girl knew she couldn't get any closer without scaring them away. She stopped, giving the little lamb another shove forward, then jumped off the trail headfirst into the deep snow.

The lamb turned, looking around for her. It let out several plaintive baas, then stood there looking around, sniffing the air. Slowly, it started making its way towards the herd of sheep. Several times it stopped and looked back for Leah. With her nowhere in sight, the lamb finally ventured to the herd where first one large ram and then each of the other adults, carefully sniffed it. The lamb stretched out its nose, as if to return their greeting. Eventually, it started moving amongst the herd, then together they all headed up the mountain, sprinting past the boulder where everyone was hiding.

CHAPTER 15

Encounter with a Grizzly

THE WOODPILE WAS GETTING LOW and it looked as though a major storm was about to move into the area. Two day's after letting Leah's lamb go, they woke to cold but crystal clear weather and Miranda and the children decided to come with Nick to get a load of wood. Before leaving, they filled the heater to the top and closed the damper so it would be warm in the tepee when they returned.

Nick and Miranda hitched the travois behind the horse, put Leah and Joseph on its back, and made their way into the forest to gather dry wood. The snow was still quite deep and it took longer than anticipated to gather a load. The birch walking stick Nick and Miranda each used helped them keep their balance as they stepped carefully on top of the softening snow. It was almost dark by the time they made their way down the path and into the open tract leading to the campsite.

They were halfway across the clearing when strange noises could be heard that seemed to be coming from behind the tepee. All at once, the head of a large grizzly appeared then a part of the tepee was knocked down as the bear thrashed about in an effort to get at the small amount of food inside. Because the wind was blowing in their face, the bear had not yet smelled them and, occupied with its mission, it had not seen them, either. Miranda grabbed her children, drawing them to her chest.

The bear took Nick by complete surprise. This time of year he had never expected to see one out from hibernation, although Jerry had said that once in a long while they do come out early. This grizzly was here because it was hungry, and a hungry grizzly was a deadly enemy.

Nick whispered for everyone to stay quiet in the hope that the bear would find the food and leave. A grizzly's sense of smell is more than one hundred times stronger than that of a human and Nick knew that at any moment, a slight shifting or easing of the light wind and the bear would be aware of their presence. He knew too, that the grizzly was an unpredictable animal but almost always went out of its way to avoid humans.

The little group of onlookers watched as the giant bear pulled down the tepee, its paws cut through the canvas wall like a razor blade. There was nothing Nick could do, the huge grizzly stood between him and the gun stored in a trunk in the tepee.

All at once the bear looked up, then casually turned back to the pile of canvas. An instant later it turned to look back in their direction. Its huge head swung back and forth like a pendulum until suddenly it bounded straight at them. Miranda and Joseph screamed while little Leah, her face ashen, stood frozen in place, gripped by a stark terror.

When the horse saw the bear coming it bolted off through the bushes, scattering the firewood as it ran. Temporarily distracted by the horse, the bear came to a halt, then rose on its hind paws and let out a horrific roar. Although thin after a long winter, the bear was still huge and its powerful front legs flailed at the air. Nick noticed one paw somehow seemed different than the other but before he could gather more thoughts, the bear lowered itself to the ground and charged.

In one hand, Nick held his hunting knife, in the other, the birch walking stick. Gripping tight the only weapons he had, he stepped forward from the others and waited for the bear to strike. When the animal was close enough, Nick swung his walking stick, grazing the huge head but it did nothing to stop its charge and the powerful bear knocked him to the ground.

Scrambling to his feet, and moving in a deliberate arc, Nick slowly distanced himself from Miranda and the children. Cautiously he edged away, all the while staring the bear straight in the eye. As he hoped, the grizzly followed, its eyes firmly focused on his movements. Believing he was far enough away from the others that the bear would be distracted enough to forget them, all at once Nick made a running dive towards the fallen tepee. Scrambling through the canvas he found the storage chest and came up with the rifle in his hands. He injected a bullet into the chamber and on his knee, took dead aim at the bear's head.

One more time the giant grizzly rose on its hind paws and let out a loud roar. Only a few yards from where he was kneeling, the bear looked straight down at him and Nick stared back, rifle aimed on target. His every instinct was to fire, to get rid of the fearsome animal that threatened their lives. But, some inner voice told him that they were the intruders, not the bear, and until the grizzly tried to attack again, he would not pull the trigger. With the gun sighted at the bear he waited while the huge creature towered above him. Huge dark eyes seemed to squint as at Nick before the animal dropped to all fours. But this time, no attack came; the giant bear quietly rambled off into the bush.

No one moved until the bear had been out of sight for several minutes. Nick walked over to a still shaking Miranda and picked up Leah in his arms. "It's okay" he assured the little girl whose trembling arms gripped his neck like the jaws of a steel vise.

"I don't think I've ever been so scared in my life," Miranda breathed the words.

Nick reached to give Joseph a reassuring squeeze of the shoulder then turned to look at the pile of debris that was their home. "I'm sorry, but it's getting dark," he put the little girl to the ground. "Your mom will take care of you while Joseph and I look after things." He looked at Joseph, hoping the frightened boy would respond.

"What do we do, Nick? Where are we going to live?" Joseph said, bewildered and still shocked from the experience.

"Don't worry, you and I will look after your mom and sister." Nick led him towards the tepee.

Although the days were warmer with the beginning of spring, in the twilight, the temperature began dropping substantially. With the increasing winds, in a short time it would be nearly thirty degrees below zero. There wasn't enough daylight left to repair the tepee so Nick and Joseph dug a hole in the snow under a large spruce tree and lined it with spruce branches. Next, they gathered up all their hides and blankets and made a bed in the hollowed-out space.

Exhausted, they ate cold beans from a can then Miranda climbed into the makeshift sleeping quarters beside Joseph and Leah. Nick covered them with blankets before crawling in next to them and they all huddled as close as possible to keep warm.

After a night of fretful sleep, at seven-thirty in the morning Nick peered out from their sleeping place and into a beautiful spring morning. A brilliant sun glistened through the trees and beads of melting snow dropped from the branches. For a brief moment, the events of the day before seemed to have been nothing more than a very bad dream. But as soon as he looked across and saw the remnants of the battered tepee, realty set in and he let out a long, slow breath. Lying next to the sleeping Miranda, her head nuzzled against his shoulder, her long black hair spilling across the side of her peaceful face, he knew then that yesterday was more than just a dream.

After a few minutes, he slipped from their sleeping place, careful not to disturb the others. Much to his elation, during the night the horse had wandered back and was standing peacefully beside the smokehouse with the travois still hitched and in tact. After disconnecting the travois and putting the horse inside the corral, he hurried to get a good fire going. Then, basking in the warmth of the bright morning sun, he checked out the damage the grizzly had done.

When Miranda and the children woke he told them it wasn't as bad as it first appeared and pointed to the horse. "Thank goodness Angel came back by herself," he told them. "Without having to spend time searching for her, if we all pitch in, we can have the tepee repaired by nightfall."

Joseph fed and watered the horse, then put on his snowshoes and gathered the wood that had been strewn about the campsite when the horse bolted. Nick showed them the grizzly's tracks in the snow where one footprint clearly indicated that a claw was missing from its left front paw. "When that old bear stood up, one paw seemed different. Now I know what it was."

"Old Broken Claw," Leah immediately dubbed it, a trace of fear returning to her voice as she spoke.

By mid afternoon, they had the frame in place and the tepee temporarily stitched together. While Miranda worked on the canvas, Nick set the stove back up. At that point, their gloom had totally disappeared from the sunny day and the progress they had made in restoring their lives. Once their beds were fixed up, the tepee, except for the bits of daylight peering through the gaps in the temporary stitching, appeared just as it always had.

That night, in the warm tepee, the tired children crawled into their beds soon after supper. Miranda tucked them in and turned out all but one of the lamps. Returning to sit near the stove, she and Nick quietly worked on repairing some torn canvas. They had been in their beds for only a few minutes when all of a sudden Leah's tiny voice broke through the dim light: "Nick, do you think old Broken Claw might come back in the middle of the night?"

"Not a chance..." Nick started to say when Joseph let out a loud roar and Leah dove under the covers.

The following days saw the weather turn even warmer, although the nights remained very cold. With the rapidly melting snow, the river started rising and the ice began breaking up. Before long, on the south slope of the hills, an abundance of fiddlehead ferns were peeking out of the ground. It was a wonderful feeling that soon they would be adding fresh greens to their diet.

Every once in a while they caught a glimpse of the grizzly that had wrecked their tepee. They knew it was the same bear because his footprints revealed the broken claw. His tracks also showed that he hadn't come anywhere near the camp again, but when they went into the woods, they could almost sense his presence and several times they did see him in the distance, watching.

With the warmer weather, they cooked some of their meals outside on an open fire. They hadn't seen Broken Claw for more than a week until one day when Nick lit the outdoor fire and he and Leah began preparing supper. He had gone inside the tepee to get some food, and when he stepped back outside Leah, who was standing by the fire, shouted over to him: "Nick, could you..." and then she froze as across the clearing a large grizzly charged straight towards her. Nick dropped the things in his arms and raced towards the girl. Leaping, he pushed her down and flung his body over hers. Covering his head with his hands, he waited for the grizzly's attack.

All at once, they heard a deafening roar and then a huge thud that sounded like two locomotives colliding. Nick looked up, grabbed Leah, and telling her to hold tight, he climbed the nearest tree. From the branches he could look down at the stream where Miranda and Joseph were washing clothes. He hollered to warn them: "Stay away from here. There are two grizzlies fighting right below us."

Nick and Leah watched as the smaller bear began losing the battle. Suddenly the bear made a run for it but the larger bear gave chase, nipping at its backside. Stopping the big bear watched as the other bear ran into the bush then it turned to look back at the campsite. The grizzly stood up on its hind legs and gave a mournful grunt, then settled back down and disappeared into the trees.

Leah cried out, "That was Broken Claw! He saved our lives!"

That was the last time they saw the big bear. Maybe he had paid his debt and moved on to a new territory. There were no new markings on the trees or any fresh tracks from that day on.

Spring arrived in all its splendor. They made it! They had survived one of the Yukon's harshest winters of the past quarter century and the time had come to dismantle the campsite. First, he took down the smokehouse and cut it up for firewood. Next, the high cache and drying racks were taken apart and burnt. Finally he buried all their garbage in a deep pit.

That night, with everything cleaned up and only the tepee and the sweat lodge still standing, an aura of sadness embraced the little group as they sat around the campfire.

"Mom, do I have to go back to school?" Joseph asked.

"Yes, you have to write your exams so you can pass into grade three next year." Miranda spoke, looking at her son who had become a young man during the past few months.

"I don't want to go back to school. The kids will fight with me."

"No, they won't," Nick told him. "Just remember what you have learned about sharing and caring for others and how to survive in the wilderness. All of that will help you to get along in the real world. Sometimes you might have to give it back first, and maybe a little harder. But remember, always give something back."

Leah laughed. "There's a boy who lives down the street from Grandma's place, and when I see him, I'm going to give him something back."

A concerned Miranda said, "I hope you guys haven't learned to become bullies!"

"No, they haven't," Nick broke in before the children could answer. "Just how to live in harmony with bullies. Love will always find a way to bring peace and contentment, even with your enemies. And in the end, they may become your friend or at the very least, respect you."

Miranda returned to the tepee and came back with a surprise, one she had managed to keep hidden from them. "Tonight, not only do you get to enjoy the campfire, but you also get c-h-o-c-o-l-a-t-e!" Miranda shouted with glee, handing each of the children a chocolate bar.

Leah and Joseph's eyes lit up and within seconds the candy disappeared.

"I can't believe how much my children have changed in the past six months," Miranda said to Nick as they sat together watching the children. "And for me, I have actually gotten to know and understand them better and to openly show them more affection. That has always been hard for me, Nick. My parents loved me yet for whatever reason I was raised without them displaying much affection," she looked at him, but he said nothing and she understood his shyness.

"You know," she continued, "I think what amazes me most is how the children have learned to get along and to share with one another. I hope they never lose that. And you Nick, I'm going to miss you very much. We will all miss you."

Joseph looked across the fire at Nick, and the realization came to the young boy that Nick would be leaving them for a long time. Trying to be brave, Joseph fought it, but tears filled his eyes as his breaking voice asked: "How long will it take you to finish your business in Vancouver?"

"I don't know for sure, Joseph. But, I promise when I do, I'll come back and visit you."

"Why can't you stay forever?" Joseph stared forlorn at the floor.

"Aren't you staying at our house?" the confused five-year-old Leah wanted to know.

Nick cleared his throat: "No not now, but who knows? Maybe some day I will." Then, mumbling that he had to go get something, a choked-up Nick Roberts, got up from his spot by the fire, and went inside the tepee.

🍃

Nick began hauling their gear to their vehicles and on his first trip was thrilled when he re-hooked his truck's battery and it started on the first try. Grateful not to have to make the nearly twenty mile horseback ride to get someone to come boost their vehicles, he loaded their things until the night before their departure there was nothing left in the tepee except a few bare essentials.

On their last morning, everyone was up early. The weather, damp and hazy, came with sporadic light drizzle. Inside the tepee, they made tea and opened the stove to toast bannock over the fire.

With breakfast over, Nick half-heartedly tied the last of their belongings on the travois. After this, all that would be needed would be one more trip to bring out the hammock and the tepee.

As they began walking out together, at the edge of the clearing they all stopped for one last look back. Along the path, they trudged single file, no one saying a word. Every so often, Nick would ask Leah if she wanted to ride on his shoulders, but she only shook her head no, and kept walking. Nick smiled at the uncharacteristic behavior of a little lady who would normally talk someone's ear off.

Joseph thought of having to go back to school, worried the boys would tease or beat him up. Miranda wondered about taking care of the children by herself; Nick's companionship and influence on them had been a wonderful thing. To her, somehow life had seemed so much easier with him around.

For his part, Nick was thinking about Leah and Joseph and how much he would miss them. He also thought about Miranda and the twenty-year difference in their ages. His feelings for her had deepened far more than he ever thought possible and leaving now seemed to be the best thing to do.

When the vehicles were loaded, everyone stood in a circle hugging and kissing each other. After a long while they broke apart, then Miranda and the children got into her car. As they drove away, Leah and Joseph waved out the back window, but Nick didn't look. He didn't want them to see him crying.

He stood there for a long time, watching the empty road. As he mounted the horse to return for the tepee, he hesitated. Climbing down, he walked back to his truck, found the tin cans and pot he wanted, then got back on the horse.

He had decided to unwind by spending one more night in the woods, sleeping in his hammock. As he sat alone by the fire he thought of their days together. Despite the dangers they had faced, here, deep in the northern wilderness he had found real family.

Never in his life had he felt such peace and now, the trees, the grass, and the river, all looked the same, but they weren't. Nothing was the same without them. Even the horse sensed something was wrong. It stood listlessly by, the hay at its feet, untouched.

Nick got up and rubbed the horse's ears. "I'm going to miss you, old girl," he told her. "If only we'd had a saddle, you would have beaten Jerry's appaloosa by a mile," he laughed and the mare seemed to nod her agreement.

Early the next morning, just as a brilliant sun edged over the eastern mountaintops, a heavy-hearted Nick Roberts let the horse run free again and headed south to the confines of a big city.

CHAPTER 16

Return to the Yukon

MORE THAN TWO YEARS after his return from the north, on a damp and rainy June morning an excited Nick Roberts loaded his things into the sleek new camper on his pickup truck, then climbed behind the wheel and left Vancouver, heading back to the Yukon. He didn't know if it was that magnificent land or his adopted family he missed the most; he only knew he needed to return.

After a full day's drive, he was still in British Columbia, making it as far north as the town of Smithers where he had arranged to stay overnight with a friend he hadn't seen in more than twenty years.

In the morning, under a clear sky, he was on the road early. Making good time, late in the afternoon of his third day on the road, Whitehorse was a welcoming sight. All around, the trees were starting to leaf green and as he thought of Miranda and the children, his mind saw the snow-capped mountains cradling the town like a mother with a newborn child.

Just as he passed the airport at the edge of town, a Boeing 737 touched down on the main runway and a smile came at the clear message that civilization had caught up with him. He continued along the highway as far as Lake Laberge, where he camped for the night.

When he pulled into Carmacks at ten-thirty the next morning, filled with excitement and more than a little trepidation, he headed for Miranda's home. He knocked on the door several times but there was no answer so he drove to the school to find the children.

He parked his car and began walking into the school playground where a group of boys were playing baseball. From behind the link fence, he watched for a few minutes until one of the youths suddenly broke from the others and raced across the field towards him. As the boy with the baseball cap sitting backwards on his head got closer, a thrilled Nick recognized the now nine-year-old Joseph Delaney.

"Holy cow, Nick! I thought that was you! How are you? How long are you staying? Can we go fishing?" The machine-gun questioning rattled from the excited schoolboy.

Laughing with a warm feeling from such a greeting, Nick said: "Hey, kid, I'm great and you're looking pretty great, too. I'd love to go fishing with you, but I'm on my way to Alaska."

Joseph made his way around the fence, reaching out to shake Nick's hand but Nick removed the ball cap, tussled the boy's hair, then stood back to take a good look. Two years could change children a lot, and Joseph had grown a few inches, thinned out even more, but the boyish grin remained.

"How come we never heard from you?" Joseph suddenly asked.

"Because I'm stupid, that's why?" He tussled the head under the baseball cap one more time. "I see you've made some friends," Nick smiled, glancing over at the group still playing ball. "Things are going good in school, are they?"

"Yup, I've got some really great buddies and my marks are so good that even my mom is pleased!" Joseph laughed.

"How is your mom? I knocked on the door but she wasn't home"

"We're at grandma's place while mom works up on the Mackenzie Delta."

"Is she still flagging for the road construction crew?"

"Oh no, mom got a job doing biology stuff."

"Really! That's great. How long will she be up there?" That Miranda had continued with her college courses and was working in her field, pleased him no end.

"All summer, I guess. But she'll be home for a little while at the end of next week. No — wait!" Joseph thought for a moment. "Not then, the one after."

"In three weeks then. Is that it?" Nick wanted to be certain.

"Yup. So how long will you be here?" Joseph repeated his question.

"Not long. I just wanted to say hello. Maybe on my way back

I'll stop and we can go fishing. School gets out for summer vacation pretty soon, doesn't it?"

"Less than two weeks and then I can fish all summer," Joseph's eyes danced at the thought of a summer in the woods.

"And where's Leah?"

"She's here, but in her classroom. Boy, she is gonna be excited to see you."

"So how do I find her?"

"Go in the front door and inside turn left down the hall to Room 228," Joseph said. Then laughing he added: "Sorry, I'm just kidding. There are only two rooms in the whole school!"

Nick was pleased at the humor, it was a great change from the insolent boy he had been when they first met. As they talked, the boys Joseph had been playing ball with started shouting for him to come back. "Hurry up, Joseph. It's your turn to bat," one of them yelled.

"I gotta go, Nick. When will I see you again?"

"I'm going to ask Leah's teacher for permission to take her off the school grounds at noon hour. If you like, you can ask your teacher and we'll all go for lunch."

"Great! I can go for sure. — Miss Walters likes me!" Joseph laughed again. "I'll meet you at the front door at twelve o'clock." He was already racing back to join his friends.

Nick walked into the school and after locating Leah's classroom, he tapped on the door and waited in the hall for the teacher.

When he introduced himself to the young redheaded woman, her face lit up immediately. "Nick Roberts, I'm glad to meet you! Leah has talked a lot about you and your winter in a tepee. She says you were the best friend she ever had," the teacher laughed. "And, she also told me that you could tell stories better than anyone else in the whole wide world."

An embarrassed Nick fumbled with his words but managed to say something about little girls with active imaginations. Explaining that he was only here for a few hours, he asked the teacher if it would be okay if he were to take Leah out for lunch.

"She will be thrilled," the woman peered into the classroom, crooking a finger.

Leah came to the door and on seeing Nick, the little girl

screamed and rushed to him, grabbing him around the waist and hugging tight.

The delighted teacher smiled at the scene then said: "Be back here at noon and don't worry about her returning to class a little late. I'm sure you guys have a lot to talk about. Miranda told me it has been a few years without hearing a word from you," the voice carrying just a polite hint of a reprimand.

"Thank you, ma'am." Nick blushed. "I'll be back a few minutes before twelve," he stroked Leah's head. Of the two children, she had changed the most.

At noon, Joseph and Leah ran to the front door where Nick was already waiting. "What would you kids like for lunch? You can have anything you want!"

"I want tons of hot bannock with fresh honey," an enthused Joseph said.

"I don't have time to make bannock," Nick laughed, tussling the boy's hair. "How about a hamburger or something?"

Leah tugged at his arm. "Nick, can we go to The Trappers Restaurant for lunch?"

"We can eat anywhere you want."

"Okay. Trappers is fine with me, too. Besides, it's the only restaurant in the whole darn village," Joseph piped in. Leah danced ahead of them, spinning as she moved.

After hamburgers and milkshakes Nick dropped the kids off at school, telling them to let their mom know that he would be stopping by when she was there in three weeks. He hugged them both then watched until they disappeared inside the school's front door. Exhilarated by his short time with them, he hopped in his truck and, whistling a tune, headed north.

Nick Roberts spent the next three weeks fishing and touring Alaska. From Fairbanks, he drove north to the end of the Dalton Highway, stopping at the tiny oilfield outpost of Prudhoe Bay on the Arctic Ocean. There, he went fishing for Arctic char before making his way back to Fairbanks. En route, he went to Manley Hot Springs, rented a camper site in the public campgrounds, and spent a few leisurely days fishing for rainbow and speckled trout in the Kantishna River. From Fairbanks he headed south to Chulitna, in the Denali National Park.

Packing a small tent, a sleeping bag, some food, and warm clothing, he started hiking up Mt. McKinley. He wasn't the only one there, a number of hiking groups passed him along the way, heading for the summit. Not ready to attempt such a challenge, even if he had the team and equipment, he was happy to pitch a tent at about the 7,000-foot level where he made dinner over an open fire. As he sat there, staring across the darkening shadows of the vast tundra, he thought of their winter spent in the Nisling Valley. Alone, high atop a bleak mountainside, his memories of Miranda and the children brought the emptiness and he longed for more times like that.

Although it was near the end of June, high on the mountain, the temperature at night dropped to ten degrees below zero. Not properly prepared for sleeping in a tent in those temperatures, he spent one of the coldest nights of his life, fully dressed, inside his sleeping bag.

Immediately at sunrise, he packed his tent and hiked down to a warmer level where he built a fire and cooked breakfast. With a full stomach, and a warm sun on his back, he leisurely made his way down the mountain and back to his truck.

After a short stop in the city of Anchorage, Nick promised himself to come back one winter to see the Iditarod Trail Sled Dog Race. At Seward he caught a ferry to Port Lions on Kodiak Island. There, he arranged for a charter boat to take him halibut fishing. The captain was an amiable fellow, and after fishing almost all day with no luck, he offered to take Nick to his own private fishing spot. In less than half an hour, he hooked onto a two hundred and fifty-pound halibut. Using only a forty-pound test line, he needed more than two hours to land the big fish.

It was late eveing by the time the fishing boat docked at the lodge. He and the captain cut up the fish and cooked two frying pans full. After their meal, Nick packed about a hundred and fifty pounds of halibut into polystyrene coolers to take back to Miranda. The rest of the fish he gave to the captain.

The next morning they met for breakfast before the captain sailed off with another boatload of tourists. Nick's ferry to Seward wasn't due to leave until two-thirty in the afternoon and with time on his hands, he went down to the pier, tossed in a line, and quickly pulled out several good-sized codfish. He filleted only one and packed it on top of the frozen halibut; the others he released.

By the time the ferry arrived, a strong cold wind was blowing from the north. The five-hour ferry trip back to Seward proved to be quite rough. A young couple, sitting across from Nick, both got terribly seasick. They spent most of the voyage going back and forth to the bathroom.

After getting off the ferry Nick drove as far as Palmer, a small Alaskan settlement, about twenty-five miles past Anchorage. There, he stayed the night at a campground on the Knik Arm of Cook Inlet. He was awake at dawn, and after washing up he stepped out of his camper to the glorious early morning sun peeking over the Wrangell mountain range. He cooked a large breakfast outdoors then, with a great deal of anticipation, headed back to Carmacks.

When he pulled up to Miranda's house, there were no cars in the driveway and no one answered his knock. Too anxious to sit and wait, he drove around the small town until he spotted Miranda's car at the grocery store. He pulled into the store's parking lot just as Miranda and the children were coming out.

Leah was the first one to spot him and came running over to his truck. Nick jumped out, picked her up, swung her around, and gave her a big hug.

"Can I ride with you back to the house?" Leah asked but without waiting for a reply the excited little girl climbed into his cab.

"Hello, Nick. It's good to see you." Despite the pleasant smile, Miranda's voice held a strong edge of reproach.

"Hi, Miranda, I'm glad to see you, too." Nick covered his nervousness by immediately asking: "I hear you are doing biology work in the Mackenzie Delta. Do you like it?"

"I like it very much," her coolness remained.

"So, how long are you home for?"

"I have the next two weeks off because the flies and mosquitoes are so bad we couldn't get any field work done. How long do you plan to stay?"

"A few days at least, but I'd like to take the children fishing on Kusawa Lake, if that's okay with you?"

"Of course, but would you mind if I and my friend Dan came along?" Miranda asked.

Caught off guard, Nick needed a moment to collect his thoughts. "Let me help you with those," he said, reaching to take some of the parcels from her arms. "Who's Dan?" he tried to sound casual.

"He's the biologist I've been working with. You'll meet him tonight."

"Is he your ah, your boyfriend?" Nick had tried to sound as nonchalant as possible.

"Sort of. We've been working together for the past three months and we get along really well."

"That's good, I'm pleased for you. I'm looking forward to meeting him. See you at the house." He turned and walked away, afraid to reveal his feelings.

"Mom, I'm going with Nick, too." Joseph said.

As soon as they arrived at Miranda's home he told her about the halibut he had caught off Kodiak Island. "I've got three full coolers for you, including one decent-sized codfish," he said walking to the back of his truck and opening the door to the camper.

"I bought a big chest freezer after you left — two years ago," Miranda emphasized the latter words. "There's plenty of room for the fish," she peered into one of the coolers. "I haven't had halibut for a long time. Thank you."

After putting the halibut in bags in the freezer, Nick and Miranda sat together at the kitchen table, sipping a cup of tea while the children disappeared outdoors to play. Through the window, Nick watched as a car pulled into the driveway and a man and a young girl got out. "I'm not sure," he said, looking over Miranda's shoulder, "but I think your friend might be here."

Miranda turned, then smiling, rose from her chair. "Come on, let me introduce you."

They stepped out onto the front porch where Miranda introduced Dan McTier and his daughter, Melissa.

"Hi, Nick! Pleased to meet you," Dan said in a friendly voice. "I've heard a lot about you from the whole Delaney family."

A pleasant-looking man, Dan McTier appeared to Nick to be someone in his late thirties. Tall in stature with a willowy build, he had an intelligent face that sported a bushy moustache in contrast to the prematurely balding head. "Pleased to meet you, Dan. And you too, Melissa," he smiled at the man's 12-year-old daughter

115

then turned back to her father. "I hope what you've heard wasn't all bad," Nick grinned.

"All good, I assure you," the man gave Nick a warm grin. "So, how long are you here for?" Dan asked as they walked inside.

"About a week. I'm taking the gang fishing on Kusawa Lake. Miranda said you might like to come along. I hope you and your daughter can join us?"

"We'd like to. However, Melissa has to go back to Whitehorse on the morning bus. Her mother is taking her to Vancouver for two weeks, but I wouldn't mind coming along."

With a rather sour look on her face, the young girl spoke to her father: "Do I have to go to Vancouver? I'd rather go fishing with you guys."

"Sorry, but your mom has already organized everything. I'll take you fishing when you get back," Dan promised.

"Let's move to the back yard," Miranda stepped in. "We can get the barbecue started and if Nick wants, he can do the honors."

"Sounds good," Nick led Dan and his daughter through the back door and into the yard where the lawn chairs were set up around a large patio table. From the edge of the woods, Joseph and Leah looked up and waved for Melissa to come over and play. "Tell them we are eating soon," Miranda said to Melissa as the little girl raced off.

While Nick lit the barbeque, Miranda went back into the house. A few minutes later she came out with vegetables and potatoes wrapped in foil along with a large package of T-bone steaks.

"Tonight we celebrate," she said. "I have a bottle of French red wine that I've been saving."

When everyone finished dinner, Joseph asked Nick what kind of fish were in Kusawa Lake and what kind of fishing tackle would be needed. Nick told him they would be fishing for lake trout and that he had enough tackle and bait for everyone. "All you'll need would be one or two rods, a bait can, and a sleeping bag. It might be a little crowded but there is plenty of room for Miranda and the children to sleep in the camper. If you don't object to my snoring, you can share the tent with me."

"No problem at all, Nick. I probably snore louder than you."

"He does," Miranda said, then blushed.

Early in the morning, everyone went along to see Melissa catch the bus for Whitehorse. It was right on time, pulling into the parking lot behind the grocery store at ten o'clock sharp. Melissa asked Nick if he would still be there when she got back from Vancouver. He said he would be gone, but promised that whenever he returned north, they would arrange to all go fishing together.

On the way to Kusawa Lake they stopped at the buffalo ranch to see his friends, Cliff and Virginia. Cliff was working in the garage and Virginia was watering the garden. They invited everyone into the house for a glass of lemonade. As soon as Joseph and Leah downed their drinks, they asked if they could go outside and see the buffalo. Cliff told them that when everybody was ready, he'd take them to see the buffalo in his truck.

A few minutes later, they all piled into the pickup truck and Cliff drove them out to the buffalo corral in the back field. The animals were gathered in the bushes at the opposite end of the large clearing. "They know the truck," Cliff told them, as he drove straight towards the herd.

Other than two of the larger bulls, who got to their feet and gave a couple of grunts just to let everyone know they were the protectors of the herd, the buffalo paid little attention as they drove up. The children all wanted to know if they could get out and pat the animals but Cliff said that was too risky. "But maybe," he said, inching the truck forward until one of the buffalo was right beside the window. "There you go," Cliff whispered and Leah and Joseph together leaned out the window and patted the huge animal. As they drove away, a few of the young ones ran alongside the truck, kicking up their heels and showing off.

After saying good-bye to Cliff and Virginia, they headed back up the highway, arriving at Kusawa Lake around suppertime. Finding a good spot close to the water, Nick parked the truck and they began unloading their gear. He untied the boat from the roof of his camper and with Dan's help slid it down and carried it to the shore. There, they gathered a number of good-sized stones and brought them back to the campsite where they piled them in a circle to make the perimeter for the fire. The children gathered stones too, but their small flat ones were sent skipping across the water.

Their campsite almost ready, the men undertook the final task of setting up their sleeping tent while Miranda warmed up her home-baked beans and boiled a pot of wieners.

The fishing was good in Kusawa Lake. Everyone, including Leah, caught their share. She was too small to cast a line from shore, so she did most of her fishing from the boat. After a few hours they put away their rods and hiked over to the opposite shore of the lake where they stopped and ate a cold lunch before trekking part way up the mountainside.

On their second full day, as they were making their way up a mountain gully on the eastern end of the lake, they almost came head to head with a large black bear and her cubs. The bears were on the same path but were above them, heading down to the lake. To give the bear and her cubs lots of room to go by, they circled well out of the way. Nick had learned his lesson with a grizzly and now he carried pepper spray just in case. The spray was effective in buying time to run but only if you managed to get it in the bear's eyes. But today, this mother bear was only interested in protecting her cubs as she too circled as far out of the way as possible.

For Nick, their time together at the lake ended all too quickly. Soon after their return to Carmacks, Nick had to say his goodbyes. Joseph made him promise to come back the next year. Miranda took him aside, and squeezing his arm warmly, made him promise to stay in touch. "You really hurt me, but even more, the kids," she said guiding him slowly down the road from her house. "It wasn't right just disappearing for two years without a word. The Christmas gifts were nice, but no phone call, and never a letter? Nick, you made me feel I wasn't important — we weren't important. And it hurt, a lot"

"I'm sorry," he turned to look at her, "you're right. I just needed to sort some things out but..."

"It's the past," she said. "Let's make the future right. Okay?"

"You got it," he said.

"And don't tell the kids you'll be back unless you mean it."

"I'll be back, Miranda. No matter what."

CHAPTER 17

An Angel Returns

THE YEAR AFTER the Kusawa Lake trip, Nick returned to take Joseph and Leah fishing at a place called Dalton Post. It would be a new experience for them, catching king salmon that weighed as much as fifty pounds. One of the fish Leah hooked onto almost pulled her into the river, but she refused to let go of the rod. Nick gave her a hand reeling it in, while Joseph waded out into the water and netted the huge fish. Of course, the camera came out, and permanent souvenirs for everyone were taken.

That night, while sitting around the campfire, Joseph asked Nick if someday they could go back to the Nisling Valley. The ten-year-old wanted to spend another winter there in a tepee.

"That would be a nice trip, but a whole winter might not be possible again. Your mom has Dan to think about, you guys really can't leave school, and my job seems to ask more and more of me. Maybe next year we could go there camping and set up a tent right where our camp used to be."

The children though it was a great idea, and they spent the rest of the evening making plans. The following day they fished only in the morning, keeping a careful eye on the many bears feeding on salmon in the river. In the afternoon, instead of fishing, they took the time to build a makeshift smokehouse for their catch. With the number of bears about, it wasn't a good idea to venture too far into the woods but there was enough wood close by to supply their campfire and keep the smokehouse working.

They spent three more days at the Dalton Post camp, not doing much fishing, but a lot of time relaxing by the river, watching other people. Joseph was always helping others landing fish or untangling someone's line. Nick watched the young boy going about freely helping others and thought of how much he had changed since they first met. All the hatred and anger seemed to be gone, Joseph never said a bad word about anyone. He behaved like a much older boy, but Nick understood the role he automatically had to assume without a father. Whatever small part he may have played in giving some direction, it did as much for Nick as it had for the boy. The difficult teen years would soon be upon him and Nick had every intention of staying as much involved as he could, even from a great distance. But watching Joseph's behaviour now, and seeing how well he was doing in school, filled him with enormous pride.

In Carmacks, saying good-bye this time proved to be the hardest one of all. In Vancouver, he made an appointment with a lawyer, and changed his will.

One afternoon in early January when Nick returned to his real-estate office after an appointment, the secretary told him that a woman had telephoned from the Yukon and wanted him to call her back as soon as possible. Concerned, Nick immediately dialed Miranda's number.

"Are you okay?" he asked the moment she answered.

Laughing, she told him that they were just missing him and thought they would call to personally thank him for the Christmas gifts and to find what dates he'd be coming this summer. She passed the phone to Leah and after he spoke to her, Joseph came on the line. They talked for a few minutes then Joseph said his mother wanted to speak to him again.

"Nick?" she said, her voice echoing her happiness. "Dan and I have decided to get married, and we want to know what date you could be here. Whatever day you chose, that is the date for the wedding."

"Wow, congratulations!" Nick said, a touch of longing inside. "I planned on going up there in early July, but my schedule is flexible. I can arrange to be there anytime that would suit you."

"The third Saturday in July is the best time for Dan's family. Is that okay with you?"

"Sure. Joseph said he wanted to go back into the Nisling Valley where we spent the winter in the tepee. I think if I come up there a few days before the wedding, it'll give us enough time to go camping. I mean, I don't want to interfere with your wedding plans so if it's not convenient for you, just say so."

"There are no great events going on. The Prime Minister is busy and the Queen of England sent her regrets so..." Miranda laughed easily, "It's going to be a small wedding. You know — just family and a few important friends."

A smiling Nick Roberts hung up his office phone, rose from his chair and left to spend the rest of the day scouring the stores for exactly the right wedding gift.

The next few months passed quickly. Four days before the wedding, Nick flew from Vancouver to Whitehorse, rented a car, and arrived in Carmacks by about three o'clock in the afternoon. Joseph and Leah were out of school and Dan's daughter, Melissa, was there for the wedding.

Excited children had Miranda pack their things for their camping trip well in advance of his arrival. After a cup of tea they were ready to leave when Melissa came in, wanting to know if she could come camping, too.

Nick glanced over at the girl's father who nodded his approval. "Of course you can come with us. We wouldn't dream of leaving you behind," Nick told her.

Taking time to enjoy the scenery, they meandered along the highway, eventually parking the car at the end of the old mine road. From there, they hiked through the woods to the spot where their winter camp used to be. The moment they stepped out of the path and into the clearing, Nick's heart leapt at the flood of memories.

"Look! Leah shrieked. "The sweat lodge is still there." And she raced towards it with Joseph and Melissa in hot pursuit.

As Nick approached, all smiles, Joseph said: "Wow, Nick. Take a look. We can still use it!" the boy shook his head in amazement.

They wandered around for a while, pointing things out to Melissa, the children telling her of various events. "And the grizzly that attacked us? He was a hundred feet tall," Leah assured her and a nervous Melissa moved closer to Nick.

When they finally got around to setting up the tents, they put their things inside and then built a roaring fire to heat the rocks for the sweat lodge.

"I just thought of something, guys." Nick said. "I don't have a towel. Do you?"

The children checked their bags and found two towels their mother had packed. While Nick and Joseph wandered down to the stream the two girls went into the sweat lodge. As they made their way along the path, they suddenly stopped to listen. In the distance behind them, they could hear singing.

By the time Nick and Joseph came back the girls were already dressed. Leah offered Nick her towel and although large enough, it was soaking wet. He told Joseph to go ahead and enjoy the sweat lodge and to sing at the top of his voice. While Nick prepared supper for them, Joseph relaxed in the steam and sang. The girls held their ears.

Later everyone sat around the fire, telling stories about what they had done during the past year. Joseph said he had begun teaching Leah and Melissa about the plants, the trees, and all the animal tracks he'd found. Nick watched and listened with great interest, then asked Joseph where he had learned everything.

Joseph said that because of their winter together he had become curious and wanted to know more about his ancestor's lives. He said that he found books at the Carmacks Branch Library and his teacher had obtained other books for him to read about the Canadian north, the different Native tribes, and their culture. Now, he wanted to share that knowledge with the girls.

For all of them, even Melissa who had never spent a night in the woods before, the three days went by quickly and soon they were heading back home.

Before the wedding, Nick met the children's paternal grandmother for the first time. Losing her son in an accident had been a terrible blow for the elderly widow but it was easy to see that her grandchildren were her pride and joy. She was pleased to see Miranda remarry so that Leah and Joseph would have a man in their life. "Full time," she said, giving Nick a friendly nudge with a sharp elbow.

The wedding was a larger affair than anyone had expected. In a small town like Carmacks, everybody just shows up. Although Miranda had plenty of food, much more came with the uninvited guests who appeared, laden with trays of sandwiches, cakes, pies and other sweets. Others showed up with bowls of salads, pots of stew or baked beans, and in the end, the house was filled with the aroma of most every dish known to man. Five local musicians appeared, ate great quantities of food, then played until three in the morning.

The next day, with all the hoopla over, Nick told Joseph and Leah he had a surprise for them and told them to follow as he walked towards the truck. Melissa, now a regular part of the children following Nick, was the first one to jump in. He drove about a half a mile west of the town before turning into a small farmyard. He stopped the car and asked the children to cover their eyes. Joseph did as he was told, but the giggling girls both peeked between splayed fingers, laughing hilariously. A grinning Nick waited until they settled down then made them promise not to peek.

"It's a grizzly bear that's gonna eat Melissa," Leah burst into laughter.

Nick's voice broke the frivolity: "Okay guys. Everyone except Leah can open their eyes."

Leah's hands instantly flew from her face, then back on, then back off. She and Joseph stared, saying nothing until it finally sunk in. "Where did you find her?" Joseph screamed, opening the car door and running towards the farmer's corral. Leah was only one step behind.

"The outfitter was using her to pack supplies up to his mountain camp," Nick said when he caught up to them by the fence.

"And...And....And," Leah's eyes flashed in anticipation.

"Yes," Nick smiled. And the child danced.

Melissa did not understand. "I don't get it," she said to Joseph.

The boy was grinning ear to ear. "Remember the horse we told you about? That's her. That's Angel." He turned to Nick. "Are we going to keep her?"

"We are, we are!" Leah climbed to stand on the fence.

"You sure are," Nick told the boy, "so long as you both are willing to take good care of her. I've paid for a year's boarding here at the farm and your mom said she will bring you out on weekends for riding lessons," Nick said then added: "Anyone want to ride her now?"

A chorus of yeses came loud and Joseph climbed the rail beside his sister, making a clicking sound with his mouth to call the horse over.

Nick went and got the farmer's equipment and saddled the horse. He helped the kids take turns riding her. Joseph and Leah rode by themselves, but Melissa would only ride if Joseph went on the horse with her.

"They have an excellent instructor here who can teach you how to ride really well," he told them as they drove back home. Miranda was waiting on the porch, all smiles at the secret she had kept from the children.

Nick stayed around Carmacks for another two days, helping the children with the horse. Before leaving, he showed them how to saddle the horse, how to get on and off by themselves, and how to change leads as they rode. He also had them muck out the horse's stall, just to understand it wasn't all play.

Chapter 18

Visiting Inuvik

JUST AS HE STEPPED IN THE DOOR from his morning work-out at the gymnasium, the phone rang in Nick Roberts' Vancouver apartment. He picked it up, assuming it was someone from the office. To his delight, the voice on the other end of the line was that of Joseph Delaney. The boy wanted to say hello and confirm the date when Nick was coming north.

"I'll be heading up on Friday, the sixth of July, but this time I'm not going to make the long drive. Instead, I'll fly into Whitehorse and rent a car. That way, I should be at your place by mid afternoon."

"Leah and I will be at our Grandma's. Meet us there, okay?" Joseph told him.

"Is everything all right? Where's your mom?"

"She and Dan are working up near Inuvik."

Relieved that there was nothing wrong, he said: "So, which house is your grandmother's place?"

"You known when you first come into town? It's the bright yellow one on the left with all the flower boxes."

Driving a rusty old half-ton pickup truck, Nick was a few hours late when he pulled into the driveway of the small wooden bungalow. An anxious Joseph was sitting on the front steps, waiting. The boy stared for a minute until his face lit up in recognition and he raced to the truck door: "Wow, where did you get this beast?" he laughed, leaning inside to look at the cab interior.

"And it's nice to see you, too!" Nick said.

"Sorry, Nick. I'm glad to see you." The eleven-year-old apologized.

"It doesn't look like much, does it? But, I call her my go-any-where truck. We can beat the heck out of it, and it won't matter.

And, it will get us through all the rough backcountry roads with no problem at all."

"I thought you were flying up?"

"I did, but I bought it from a guy I met at the airport in Vancouver. He was on my flight to Whitehorse and told me he was moving south permanently. Turns out he had this old truck and was glad to find a buyer before he left. Not bad for five hundred bucks, eh!" Nick patted the dash.

"I think it's pretty neat." Joseph grabbed the box side and with one leap, swung himself up, landing flat on his feet in the bed of the pickup.

"Now, that was pretty neat!" Nick leaned out the window to speak. "Where's Leah?"

"Riding lessons."

"What say we go see her?"

"Sure," Joseph jumped to the ground.

"Let's go tell your grandmother, first."

At seven in the morning, under an overcast sky, the three of them were packed and on their way up the Klondike Highway in Nick's battered pickup. At the head of the Mackenzie Delta, the town of Inuvik was where Dan and Miranda were based for their summer job. As the old truck rattled past Pelly Crossing, charcoal fields and stumps of trees marred the landscape where a bushfire had swept through just days before. Because of still-smoldering hot spots, in certain places the smoke became so thick that the highway was barely visible.

They had to detour west as far as Rock Creek to get fuel, then double back and head straight north up the Dempster Highway. They followed the North Klondike River for two hours, climbing several thousand feet up the side of Mt. Jecknell where amazed children watched as the truck broke through the clouds. Following steep mountainous terrain, around sharp switchbacks that slowed their progress, on the first day they made it as far north as Eagle Plains.

At the campground behind the lodge, they set up their tent and cooked dinner over an open fire. As they ate, Joseph told Nick that they were moving to Whitehorse in September in time for him and Leah to start school there. He said he didn't want to go to school in Whitehorse because he was afraid the kids would tease him like they had when he first went to school in Carmacks.

Nick though for a moment before he spoke. "It's always tough going into a strange environment. Just remember what you have learned from your past experience at school plus what you know about surviving in the wilderness. If you can survive there, you can survive anywhere."

"It's not a case of survival. It's a case of the kids liking me and getting along with me." Frustration showed in the boy's voice.

"I like you and I think you're a pretty nice fellow. Why wouldn't everyone else like you?"

"Nick, that's different."

"Well, Joseph, maybe not. If you start off with a positive attitude about everyone in your new school, most likely they'll all be glad to accept you as a friend."

After further discussion with Nick, Joseph seemed to be a little more at ease about the change.

"As an adult, you will have to face new environments fairly often, Joseph. When you go to university and when you take on your first job are just two examples. What's important is to maintain the right outlook."

Leah, who had been unusually quiet, spoke up: "I'm not afraid to go to school in Whitehorse. I can hardly wait to make new friends."

Without noticing it, their campfire had almost burned itself out. Nick yawned, looked at his watch, and for a moment thought it was broken. Shortly before midnight, here in the Yukon, the sun was still shining.

Before Leah and Joseph opened their eyes, Nick had a breakfast ready of eggs, baked bannock, store-bought honey, freshly picked cattail shoots, and Labrador tea. As soon as they finished eating, they packed up their things and began taking down the tent.

Nick's large new tent, made from space-age materials, had a privacy divider which he understood that for the nearly ten-year-old Leah, had become very important. Lightweight, and moisture proof, he could tuck it under one arm and carry it almost anywhere. New technology, which he frequently complained about in the big city, did have its advantages here in the wilderness.

After driving across the Richardson Mountains, just past Fort McPherson the land flattened out but the roads were still windy and bumpy. When the trio arrived in Inuvik it didn't take long to find Dan and Miranda's temporary living quarters in the government complex at the outskirts of the town.

A very pretty teenager in a pastel blue dress came bounding out to meet them. For a second Nick stared, wondering who the girl with the short blonde hair, eye shadow, and bright red lipstick, might be. When she spoke, he understood. In one year, Dan's daughter had blossomed from an awkward teenager into a beautiful young lady.

Melissa said she had flown in from Whitehorse that morning and wanted to know if she could go back with them when they left. Nick said there was room in the king cab, so if her father approved, she could. Looking at her from head to toe he added: "Only thing is, you might want to dig out your old jeans. It gets pretty dusty in my old truck."

Dan and Miranda appeared, and after the hugs, Miranda brought them all inside and asked Nick if he wanted to freshen up. After a quick shower, and strong tea, they sat around talking about the year gone by. Dan said that he and Miranda had booked a week off work and had made arrangements to take him Arctic char fishing. "Where we are going is full of wildlife, including beluga and bowhead whales, and maybe even a few ringed seals."

It was exactly the kind of trip Nick enjoyed and it turned out to be even better than he had expected. Although technically a vacation, Dan and Miranda would still spend time collecting data on some of the animals along the way. As such, their boss authorized the use of the government's thirty-two-foot Bayliner. With a lot of sleeping area and a big galley, it made for a pleasant trip but just as important was that out on the Beaufort Sea, the powerful boat could safely handle the rough waters.

Everyone was excited as they pitched in to load all the supplies. It was a sunny and calm morning when Dan slowly guided the boat up the east channel towards Kugmallit Bay.

About two and a half hours later, they passed the Indian village of Turunuk and charted northeast along Richards Island. The land, flat and treeless, was covered with all kinds of grass and vivid wildflowers. Dan let the boat drift so they could all take in the sight of hundreds of caribou grazing on the tundra along the banks of the channel. At one point during the trip, they watched as a caribou herd thundered along the bank then plunged into the water and began swimming across the bay.

"Look," Miranda pointed to the frustrated wolf pack that stood on the bank, watching its prey get away.

The channel was filled with the abundance of wildlife Dan had promised. This time of year, the Canada geese, eider ducks, mallards, and other waterfowl all had young ones trailing behind. As the boat approached, the protective parents would flop clumsily across the water, pretending to be injured, trying to lure away anything that might harm their babies.

It was ten o'clock at night when they tied up at the dock in Kittigazuit. The sun was high on the horizon but even in the broad daylight, after their long day on the water, everyone was ready to turn in.

The next day, they crossed Kugmallit Bay to Tuktoyaktuk, where a friend of Dan and Miranda's lived. They asked some kids playing on the docks if anyone knew where they could find Gilbert Howe's residence.

One of the boys said, "Gilbert went out on his boat this morning but his wife is home. I'd be glad to show you where they live — she bakes the best cookies in the world!" the teenager grinned.

It was about a ten-minute walk from the docks to where Gilbert lived and his wife Amanda welcomed them in. The boy who had brought them stood by the door, not moving and a smiling Amanda Howe went to her large pantry and brought out a container of oatmeal chocolate-chip cookies. The boy thanked her, stuffing his pockets with as many cookies as he thought the good-hearted woman would allow. After he raced off to rejoin his friends, Amanda turned and said to Dan and Miranda: "You have to stay until Gilbert gets home, I know he would love to see you. It won't be too long, he just went out to lift his nets."

"Thank you, as long as we're not disturbing you?" Dan said.

"Disturbing me? Believe me, way out here I'm always glad to see a new face. A cookie anyone?" she said, reaching into the open container.

An hour later, her husband came through the door. When Gilbert Howe saw their guests, a big smile came as he was introduced to Nick and the three children. "What a nice surprise to meet your kids. When I saw the government boat at the dock, I figured it had to be you guys. Oh, by the way, I've got a box of fresh fish for you to take back. It's on my boat but I packed it in ice already."

When Dan and the others rose to leave, Gilbert insisted they stay for dinner. Hospitality was a way of life and not to accept an invitation to dinner, an insult. Amanda Howe prepared a sumptuous caribou roast with all the trimmings and everyone was glad they stayed — particularly when she brought out dessert.

After dinner, they all walked down to the docks to get the fish Gilbert had for them and as they did, a dozen kids from the village appeared, tagging along. Curious about the government boat, Dan invited the children aboard and they all took turns sitting in the captain's chair. Seeing how excited they were, Dan started up the motor and took them for a ride around the bay. It was well after eleven o'clock when they said goodnight.

At seven o'clock in the morning, Gilbert was back at the docks. This time, he had a box of smoked fish under his arm. "You gotta try this," he said. "It just came out of the smokehouse. You can eat it along the way." After they thanked the man again for his hospitality and thoughtfulness, they untied the boat and got underway.

The trip onto the Beaufort Sea was one filled with excitement. In the afternoon, they saw a pod of eight bowhead whales and for almost twenty minutes watched as four Belugas swam along the bow of their boat. A short time later, they spotted a polar bear and her cub walking along the shore on Pelly Island. Dan slowed the boat so they could all get a better look and Nick dug out his camera.

Their travels took them through the Mackenzie Bay and finally down the middle channel, back to Inuvik. Along the way, Nick had been able to relax on a deck chair, taking in the scenery, and listening with great pride as Miranda talked about her biology work.

CHAPTER 19

Nick and Joseph Explore the Yukon

O VER THE NEXT FEW YEARS, Joseph was the only member of his family to go on the trips. Leah was changing, a young teenager expanding her interests with new friends and new things to do. But it all happened as a part of the natural process of growing and although he sometimes wished it didn't, Nick Roberts understood.

For Joseph Delaney, a week or so each summer camping with Nick was important, and as he grew older, he too understood something: their time together was just as important to Nick. A very responsible young man, Joseph would plan every detail of their trip months in advance and was always ready to go as soon as Nick landed in town.

For more than eleven months of the year, the old truck Nick had bought sat rather forlorn in their yard. Each summer, just before he was due to show up, the mechanic from the local garage dropped by, checked it out, and got it running. The truck wasn't really a very sound investment. The insurance costs and the annual tune-up, that most always came with a hefty bill for a worn-out part, was an awful lot to spend for a few weeks out of the year. But the truck seemed to give Nick a special pleasure and Joseph had to admit that he too had a strange pride in the battered old Chevy.

Joseph had just celebrated his fifteenth birthday the summer he and Nick hiked into the Hess Mountains. At fifteen, he was already nearly six feet tall and although slender, he was powerfully built. For this trip, he had the tent, the sleeping bags, and all the gear loaded in the back of the old truck long before Nick arrived. Even the canned food was packed; only the small amount of fresh food remained to be loaded.

They drove southeast on the Alaska Highway as far as Johnson's Crossing at the end of Teslin Lake. From there, they

131

headed due north. After passing the town of Ross River and following the river itself north, the road became narrower and rougher the farther they drove into the mountains. The trail eventually took them along the east side of Mt. Sheldon, then wound its way towards MacMillan Pass running next to the dried-up bed of the South MacMillan river. Before reaching the steep incline of the Pass, they were driving on what was only a shell of a road, and it was then that they got the truck hung up on a large boulder. When they got out to check, they found three wheels were completely off the ground. The only way to get it free was to jack it up and put enough rocks and gravel under the wheels to clear the boulder that it was resting on.

The weather all day had been sunny and hot, but as they worked to free the truck, dark clouds started moving in from the west. Soon there were lightning flashes and loud cracks of thunder all around them. Before they could get the truck free from the boulder the skies opened and the rain poured down. They had to stop working on the truck and with the cab full of gear, they had no choice but to set up the tent. Although they were both soaking wet, with all the hard work neither of them were cold. They hung a tarp over the front of the tent to shield them from the rain and Nick eventually managed to get a fire lit and burning well enough for them to dry off a little before going to sleep.

The lightning and thunder continued all through the night and strong winds rattled the sides of the tent. At about five-thirty in the morning a bolt of lightning struck a tree just a few yards away from their tent. The tree came crashing down, landing between the tent and the truck. A thick branch smashed through the pickup's windshield and the outer limbs of the large tree flattened their tent. They were lucky to get out of there with only a slight injury to Joseph's leg.

The heavy rain had long since drowned their fire and all the wood they had gathered earlier was soaking wet. With the combination of wet wood and high winds, it was impossible to restart the fire. They covered the broken windshield with one of the wet sleeping bags and, resigned that some of it had to get wet, they moved some of their gear from the cab to the back of the truck.

Huddled in the front seat, wet from top to bottom and growing colder by the minute, time seemed to stand still. When Nick lit a match and checked his watch, it was quarter past six. He whispered to Joseph, "Are you sleeping?"

"No, I can't sleep.?"

"I wasn't able to, either. It's let up a little, so I'm going to get out and try to get a fire started." As he spoke, water dripped through the soaked sleeping bag on the windshield and onto his legs.

"I'll come help," Joseph said and they both climbed from the truck.

They cut branches from the fallen tree and used them to make a windbreak. A few yards away, to their great joy they found a parched cedar log on the ground. They chopped it into kindling and eventually got a good fire going. By the time they finished a breakfast of canned spaghetti, their spirits were buoyed further when the drizzle stopped and a warm sun poked through the clouds.

It was a good hour before they managed to get the truck off the boulder, turned around, and facing back down the mountain. They had pushed their luck and paid the price for trying to drive too far into the hills. This spot was where the truck would sit; the rest of the way up the mountain would have to be on foot.

Dry for the first time in many hours, and filled with a solid breakfast from their second meal that morning, their spirit soared as they climbed the mountain. Just before reaching the summit of the MacMillan Pass they smelled smoke and stopped to look around. Below them, but not all that far away, they could see a fire rolling up the mountain pass. Lightning had ignited a blaze on the mountain that had gained enormous strength as it ate up the brush and tinder below them.

They understood that they had to get out of there as fast as possible. They veered wide, trying to gauge the path of the fire. When they finally made their way down to where they had left the truck, they could see the fire burning between themselves and the river.

Nervous, and uncertain as to how fast the fire was traveling, Nick edged the truck through smoke so thick at times he could barely discern the road. Bits of ashes and burning embers, scattered by the winds, were falling all around them yet they had no real idea exactly where the fire was burning. Suddenly, Joseph shouted out that the river was there in front of them. What had been a dry riverbed on the way up, was now filled with more than two feet of swirling water surging its way down over the rocks.

Nick drove the truck into the middle of the waterway, then he and Joseph jumped out. Hidden by all the smoke, they had not seen that some of their cardboard boxes in the back had already started burning. It was a minute or two before they noticed, and using their hands, they splashed water over the boxes until the fire went out. To try to save what was left, they wet down the remaining supplies. Too tired to be afraid, they sat down in the water near the truck.

Although they ducked under the water repeatedly, Nick got burned on the face from a flying ember. They were in the middle of the fire's path and the concentration of heavy smoke from the burning stumps darkened the sky so much that it seemed like night. After two harrowing hours of sitting in the river the front of the fire had burned over them and was heading up the pass. They water level began dropping and they felt they were better off if they left. Climbing back in the truck, the soaked duo held their breath, then let out a disappointing sigh as the truck's wet ignition gave only a click when Nick turned the key. From under the seat he pulled out a dry rag and, opening the hood, he wiped off all the wires, then removed the distributor cap and did his best to dry out the rotor. When he put it all back together, Nick climbed behind the wheel and put his hand on the key.

"Say a prayer to Mary, Joseph." Nick laughed, wanting to ease the tension. They both broke into a wide smile when the engine roared to life. Afraid to get stuck in the soft river bottom, he gently backed the old truck out, making sure not to spin the wheels.

On high ground, he stopped and looked at Joseph, concerned that the traumatic events might have taken a toll on someone so young. "Are you okay?"

"I'm fine, Nick. — As long as no darn grizzly shows up!"

A smiling Nick Roberts jammed the old truck into gear and started down the road. By the time they reached the Ross River, the fire seemed to have burned itself out. Fairly certain they were now safe, they camped there for the night, anxious to get dried out. Fortunate that the holes in the tent could be easily patched, once they had dried a change of clothing over a fire, they set up the tent on a high spot close to the river and got an uneasy night of sleep.

Waking to a crystal clear morning, the smoke, now in the far distance, had all but dissipated. Nick got the breakfast fire going while Joseph ran a rope between two trees and hung the things out to dry.

As they sat eating their meal, Joseph looked up, pointing. "Wow, look at the snow on the top of the mountain."

Nick looked at Mt. Sheldon, then at Joseph, and he knew exactly what the boy was thinking. "Not too tired?" he asked.

"No, I'm good to go," Joseph assured him then realized what Nick was saying. "Tomorrow," he added, "today we need to relax and dry things out — me included." He stretched out on the ground, basking in the warmth of the summer sun.

Rejuvenated, the following morning they packed their gear and with enough food for three days, they headed up the mountain. The first part was fairly easy going but it wasn't long before the mountain started getting the best of them. As they picked their way up the steep cliffs, a cloud moved in around them, lowering visibility to less than ten feet and making the rocks slippery and dangerous to climb. In those conditions they were unable to go any farther. Not wanting to chance climbing down, they spent the night on a small rocky ledge.

When they awoke, the clouds had all moved off the mountain. They were able to climb up another two thousand feet bringing them as far as the snow line. In the cool crisp air, they lit a fire and ate a hearty lunch. After, they explored the mountain, taking in the view, pointing out this and that to each other as they did. The past turmoil and danger vanished from their mind, replaced by the peaceful magnificence of the splendor around them.

The next day they descended to where they had left the truck and all too soon were back in Whitehorse.

CHAPTER 20

Old Friends and New Places

O N A BEAUTIFUL JUNE MORNING, Nick Roberts walked from the parking lot to his real-estate office, lost in thought about the big transaction that was scheduled to close that day. The moment he entered the front door, the secretary told him to call Joseph Delaney as soon as possible.

"Did he say anything else?" an alarmed Nick asked.

"No, Mr. Roberts. Only for you to call ASAP."

An uneasiness swept over him, and he rushed to his office. Tossing his briefcase on his desk, he picked up the phone and dialed the Delaney's home phone number.

After the third ring, a young male voice said "Hello."

"Joseph? It's Nick. What's wrong?"

"Nothing. Why?"

Nick breathed a sigh of relief. "I was just a little concerned. What's up?"

"I phoned to tell you that Mom bought me my own horse. His name is Whisper and he can run like the wind."

"That's really great! Did something happen to Angel?"

"No, she's terrific. Leah rides her all the time."

"So tell me about Whisper the wonder horse," Nick chuckled.

"Your friend Jerry Beaumont was here and he came out to the ranch with me to pick out the horse. He said it's the best one he'd ever seen."

Nick's mind stopped, switching to memories that had seemed so long ago. It had been years since he'd last seen his friend. "Jerry's an expert, so if he says so, Whisper must be something special. By the way, how's Jerry doing?"

"He's just fine. In fact, he's running a dude ranch at his place in Stony Creek. He told me to ask you if you would like to visit him this summer."

"Absolutely."

"Jerry says we could come along with him on a trail ride. It sounds like a really good trip. He does a ride into Hutshi then cuts across the mountain to his camp at Aishihik. We'd be riding with other guests, and he can always use a couple of wranglers to help out along the trail. Are you interested?"

"Sounds like a lot of fun. Speak to Jerry and let me know when."

"As soon as I find out more, I'll give you a call."

"How's your mom?" Nick asked, and they caught up on family doings before hanging up.

A few weeks later, Joseph phoned back to tell Nick that Jerry Beaumont had a weeklong trail ride booked on the dates Nick would be there. "Mostly city folk, Jerry said to tell you!" and Joseph laughed.

"I'm really looking forward to it," Nick enthused before he hung up and immediately dialed his travel agent's number.

He booked a flight from Vancouver to Whitehorse that would give him a few days to visit Dan and Miranda before going to Jerry's place. Wanting to do a little fishing after the trail ride, he reserved his return flight for a week later.

When Nick arrived at the Whitehorse airport, to his surprise, Joseph was waiting for him at the gate.

"Are you alone?" Nick asked as they made their way out of the terminal.

"Yup," Joseph could barely contain his excitement.

"How did you get here?"

"With the truck." He tried to say it as matter-of-fact as possible.

"You drove?" A proud smile spread across Nick's face.

"I sure did. Got my driver's license a month ago!" Joseph beamed.

"Well, in that case, I'd be pleased to have a chauffeur take me to the Delaney estate!" Nick teased.

The old truck was spotless, even the rust spots had been patched and primered. Tossing his bag in the back, Nick climbed into the passenger's seat and buckled his seat belt.

"I had the garage put in a new windshield, but I did the tune-up myself."

"I'm impressed, young feller." Nick reached over and rubbed the boys head, something he hadn't done in years. It was only driving a beat up old truck, yet this was a very special trip as Nick watched Joseph maneuver slowly out of the parking lot. On the highway, the diligent teenager maintained a steady forty miles an hour.

"Nick, let's go see my horse. You can ride him, and I'll ride Angel."

"I think we should say hello to everybody before we go galloping off. And I do have to change my clothes."

"There's nobody home. Mom and Dan won't be back until five o'clock, and Leah is at her friend's place. She said to call her as soon as you got here. We can go for a little ride first and call her when we get back."

"All right then. Let me get changed and we can go see this super-horse."

Joseph was proud as punch showing Nick his horse. A big, but gentle chestnut gelding, it was indeed a majestic animal. Joseph had bought a good second-hand saddle and bridle. He told Nick he'd worked at all kinds of odd jobs to earn the money.

Nick had intended that it be just a short ride, but once out on the trail, time had no meaning and it was more than three hours later when the two elated riders returned home.

The morning of their departure for Jerry's place, they went to the stable where they attached the borrowed horse trailer behind the truck and loaded Joseph's horse. After packing their supplies, they said good-bye to everyone and headed for Stony Creek.

When they pulled into the yard, Jerry Beaumont was leaning up against the corral fence watching the horses. His head turned and a wide smile came at the sight of them.

Jerry greeted Nick warmly, then promptly gave him heck for not visiting before this.

Pointing to one of the horses in the center of the corral, Jerry said: "That big gray over there? That's the one you're gonna ride, Nick. I can't seem to get anyone to stay on him. Every time I send him out with a rider, he comes back by himself."

"I'm here two minutes and you want to get me killed already!" Nick laughed.

"No such luck," Jerry scoffed, a wide grin made the huge moustache twitch. "I think you can handle him."

"How many people do you have going on the ride?"

"There's supposed to be fifteen, altogether. Six men and nine woman, plus you, me, and Joseph. With all of us plus the six pack-horses it's gonna be the biggest ride I've ever had. It should be fun."

"This is a tough trip. Are your customers aware of that?" Nick asked.

"I run different kinds of rides. Some for raw beginners and others like this where they must be experienced. Most are from the city and don't ride often so they come here for a real treat, riding in the wilderness."

It was quarter after six in the morning when cars started pulling into the yard. As soon as the paying guests had unloaded their sleeping bags and personal gear, each was assigned a horse according to their size and riding ability. While Jerry and Joseph were busy loading the supplies onto the packhorses Nick served coffee to the people who stood around talking excitedly about the adventure ahead.

Jerry rode at the front of the pack, waving his hat and beckoning for everyone to follow. Joseph rode midway in the group, while Nick brought up the rear, riding the big gray and leading the packhorses. The morning began under cloud with a hint of rain, but the skies cleared by ten o'clock. By that time, the riders had spread out to almost a half a mile in length. When Jerry noticed that some of the riders weren't keeping up, he stopped and told the small group with him to dismount and stretch their legs.

When they all finally caught up, Jerry rode back to the middle of the pack and stopped about twenty feet away. He stood on his saddle, looked up and down at the group and shouted so all could hear. "It's important to stay close to the rider in front. We have to keep together or somebody's going to get lost. I'm going to slow down a little, but we want to make it as far as Hutshi tonight. If anybody has a problem, let me know." He paused looking up and down the row of riders again. "Any sore bums?"

A dozen hands shot into the air.

When they stopped for lunch, Jerry boiled a pot of tea and opened several large cans of beans. Nick poked fun at his friend:

"Hey, Jerry, I hope you brought more to eat than just beans and bread."

"You know Nick, by the time this trip is over, those beans will be tasting pretty good," Jerry whispered, the mocking grin etched in his face.

When the group arrived at their destination for that evening, Jerry once again rode to the middle of the pack to address the group. "Folks, let me tell you a little bit about this place. What you see is the remnants of an old Indian village named Hutshi. At one time, it was a thriving community, home to more than two hundred people. The village was what we refer to as a Crow settlement. That's because there were two clans of the Southern Tutchone tribe. In one, the male heads of the family were called Crow, and in the other the male heads of the family were called Wolf. They were not allowed to marry into their own clan, a Crow had to marry into the Wolf clan and a Wolf had to marry into the Crow clan. The Crow families lived along the lake and the Wolf families lived farther back. When the first white man's trading post was built in the area in the early 1900's, people gradually moved away. Within forty or fifty years, there was no one left. Now, the only thing to see are the scared burial houses. Please respect this land and enjoy your stay. Thank you for your attention."

Setting up camp for eighteen people was a big task but Jerry had been here days earlier organizing the site. After a dinner of pan-fried shrimp, fresh potatoes and vegetables cooked on the metal grill, Jerry walked around speaking to each of his guests, answering their questions and accepting their compliments on the evening meal. "My friend Nick prefers beans," Jerry told them, "but I kinda go for the shrimp."

Sitting around the fire, he cautioned everyone about the danger of bears. "You are now in bear country. Although at this time of year they usually stay at a higher elevation, sometimes they will come down this low looking for food. Always be alert for them and before going out of the tent at night to answer the call of Mother Nature, listen first and check the horses. They can smell if a bear is around and they get jittery. If the horses are calm, you're pretty safe."

"Safe or not safe, I'm sure not going out in the night," the lady accountant from Lodi, California said.

"Me either," another woman piped up and they all laughed when one of the men, a strapping six foot engineer from Calgary, said he wasn't setting foot outside his tent at night.

Roasting marshmallows they talked and told jokes until the petite blonde girl from Seattle unpacked a guitar and in a lonely, haunting voice, began singing a country ballad. They urged her to sing more and when the night was over, everyone made a point of complimenting her on her beautiful voice.

The next day took them on an old Indian trail over Red Granite Mountain to the south end of Aishihik Lake. The trail was steep and narrow with many switchbacks. Every half-hour they had to stop, dismount, and rest the horses.

Although trees were few and far between, large boulders blocked the view of the trail both ahead and behind. At the back of the pack, Nick was struggling to keep the packhorses in line when all of a sudden a horse went galloping past, dragging its rider. He let go of the packhorses, pulled on the right rein, and dug in his spurs urging the horse on. The big gray spun around and leapt forward, charging after the runaway. Nick quickly pulled up alongside and reached over to grab the reins. Bringing the horse to a standstill, he jumped off and reached down to touch the prostrate woman, her leg still caught in the stirrup.

She looked up at him and groaned. Her face was covered with blood from a gash on the forehead. After he freed her foot from the tangled stirrup, he began checking for broken bones. As he bent over her, Joseph came riding up, clutching the packhorses. Almost immediately, a horrified Jerry arrived on the scene.

Nick told him the woman had fallen from her horse and had been dragged. One look at her and Jerry rushed to get a canteen of water and the first-aid kit from the saddle on one of the packhorses. He handed a dampened cloth to Nick who carefully began wiping the blood from the woman's face.

"Is she going to be all right?" another rider asked as soon as he rode up.

The woman herself spoke. "I'll be okay, I'm sorry."

"Don't be sorry," Nick said.

"One of the other riders told me a bear spooked her horse," the thin man in the plaid shirt told them. By then all the other riders had gathered around, nervously watching the woman.

"I think she'll be fine. Thank goodness the cut on her forehead isn't as serious as all that blood made it appear." Nick assured them. "We couldn't find any broken bones, just a few bruises on her back. She needs to rest a while before continuing."

Suddenly one of the riders turned to Nick. "You saved her life," he said and everyone went silent, listening. "This man reacted so fast, it was incredible! And he caught up to that frightened horse and got it stopped in seconds." The man looked at Nick then dropped the reins and started to clap. One by one the others followed until everyone had honored what he had done. Even the injured woman managed a smile, and she too joined in with a feeble clap. Nick Roberts wanted to hide under the nearest rock.

The woman didn't want to get back on her horse; she said she preferred to walk a little way, first. She stayed with Nick at the back of the pack and he walked beside her as the others went on ahead. Out of earshot, Joseph told the rest of the group that the woman was fine but needed to walk past the spot where she fell off the horse.

Two hours later, it was a somber group that reached the flats at the foot of the mountain. Needing to change the atmosphere, Jerry took a chance with a little psychology and suddenly yelled: "Let's go guys. I'll see you at the lake," he let out a holler and bolted away as fast as his horse could take him. All at once the others responded. The sound was deafening with all the hooting and hollering from sixteen riders and their thundering horses racing towards the lake.

That night they made their camp at the south end of the lake. The injured woman was much better, acting normal, walking about with only a slight limp. Instinctively, she stayed close to Nick, sitting next to him during their meal and at the bonfire that night.

The next day they followed a mining road along the east side of the lake that led them to Jerry's trapping camp. A big lake, twelve miles long and about a mile wide, its cold clear waters held an abundance of trout. Between everyone in the group, they had only six fishing rods, and even those who had never liked fishing, took turns catching fish for supper.

The following morning, before they made their way out, Jerry cautioned the group once again. "Today we'll be riding back along the lake where there are no trails, only bush and muskeg. Please be cautious and stay together. If anyone gets separated from the group they could end up being bear bait. Is that clear?" There was a flurry of yeses.

The woman who had been injured remained at the back, near Nick. The ride was slow and rough going in places, but they all stuck together and made it back to the north end of the lake shortly after four in the afternoon. That evening they had another singsong beside the large bonfire, and everyone felt a little sad that this was their last night on the trail.

Their final day was a long ride down to Canyon Creek, then along the highway past the village of Champagne, and back to the ranch at Stony Creek.

The small group had bonded in a short time, and as they prepared to depart everyone took the time to thank Jerry for his hospitality and Nick for his heroic effort. The woman hugged him so long that the others all laughed at his turning beet red with embarrassment.

Back in Whitehorse, Nick savored the enjoyable time spent with Miranda and Dan but was delighted when Leah offered to spend an afternoon with him riding the horses. At fourteen years of age, she was now a beautiful young girl; Miranda had said that already more than one boy from school had taken notice. Although self-confident and capable, the impish behaviour and ready giggle at the slightest thing funny remained from the little girl he had first met. After four years of not sharing any of their outdoor trips, their short time together took on a special meaning for Nick.

In the morning before leaving he and Leah took one last ride together. While Joseph sat behind the wheel of the truck waiting to take him to the airport, with real reluctance Nick said his goodbyes to everyone.

CHAPTER 21

Leah's Later Years

MUCH TO NICK'S DELIGHT, Leah began calling him once a month. Over the next four summers she still did not join the men on the excursions into the wilderness but whenever Nick visited the Yukon, the two found time to be together. What pleased him the most was the day Leah called to say she wanted to come along on their canoe trip that summer.

Joseph had told her about their plans that would take them from Lake Bennett down the Yukon River to Dawson City. Their ten-day journey, covering nearly five hundred miles, would retrace the same route the gold seekers had made more than a century ago.

Nick told Leah he was delighted she was joining them and it was then she informed him she also wanted to bring a boyfriend.

Caught off guard, he had to think. Was it possible? Yes, it was, her last birthday she had turned nineteen. He knew it was serious when she told him it was important to her that he meet and get to know Tom.

Thomas Donnelly was his name, but she called him Tom, telling Nick that they had been dating for almost a year. Nick was tempted to ask what her mother thought of this Tom fellow, but he bit his tongue and instead politely asked Leah to tell him a little about the man in her life.

She said they had met by chance at a restaurant in Whitehorse. Tom was a twenty-three year old Irishman from a family that immigrated to Canada shortly after he was born. They had been living in Whitehorse for the past fifteen years. "He graduated from university last year and worked as a Geotechnical engineer on an Alaska Highway project," she told him, great pride filling her voice.

Nick wanted to know if her boyfriend had the experience to handle a wilderness outing. Leah said that Joseph had already explained everything about the trip, and Tom was enthusiastic about coming along.

"In that case, Leah, I think I like him already!" Nick said.

"My turn," Joseph's voice broke through on the extension phone.

"Hello, young feller!" Nick gave an easy laugh.

"See you soon, Nick," Leah said. "He's all yours, Joseph." She hung up the phone.

"My sister's got it bad," Joseph said. "I suppose she told you all about her Tom."

"Yes, she did. So what's up with you? Have you decided what to do about your education?"

"I hate to think that I spent two years at Yukon College studying for a business administration diploma that I'll never use."

"I don't understand?"

"I don't know why, but my ideas have changed — a lot. I need time to think things over, but one thing for sure, offices just aren't for me."

"You're young, it's not easy. Having kids in high school make a lifelong career decision never made a lot of sense to me. But, I can't suggest any alternative."

"I feel like I'm going to disappoint both my mom and Dan, when I tell them. I'm almost twenty-one, I'm supposed to be a responsible young adult."

"Joseph, I wouldn't worry about it. They will understand, and there is still lots of time to figure things out."

"What I need is a job that let's me sit all day on the banks of a stream with a fishing rod in my hand." Joseph laughed.

"Actually, that does sound a lot better than sitting in front of a computer screen all day!"

Filled with great anticipation, Nick Roberts arrived at the Whitehorse airport where Joseph, Dan, Miranda, and of course Leah with her friend Tom, were all there to meet him. The only one missing from Nick's adopted family was Dan's daughter, Melissa. Studying for a degree in veterinary medicine, she had decided to work in Edmonton for the summer. Getting experience at an animal shelter was important because after graduation she planned to open her own clinic in Whitehorse.

That night they were all together for a back-yard barbeque. A few neighbours dropped by and Miranda introduced Nick to a new family who had just moved into the house next door. They were fascinated with Miranda's story of their winter in the wilderness and asked Nick to tell them more.

Early in the morning Nick and Joseph loaded the canoes and all the supplies into the back of the old pickup truck. Leah's friend Tom showed up at six-thirty, and before long the house was a beehive of activity as they prepared to leave. Dan and Miranda were driving them to Bennett Lake and would pick them up ten days late in Dawson City. With six adults, two canoes, and several hundred pounds of gear, they had to take two vehicles in order to transport everything.

Within half an hour of their arrival at Bennett Lake, they were on their way. Miranda and Dan stood on the shore waving, watching until the canoes were almost out of sight.

Nick and Leah followed in one canoe while ahead, Joseph coached Tom on balance and rhythm. Tom had paddled a canoe a few times but the protective Joseph wanted to make certain he could handle one properly before seeing him ride alone with his sister.

Within a few hours of their departure, the skies darkened and a light drizzle with a steady headwind moved in, making for very slow going. Rather than stay on the water under the wet and windy conditions, they decided to set up camp along the shore and warm themselves beside a good fire.

Just after dawn on their second day, they paddled through the narrow waterway of Miles Canyon. With its steep rock walls, the gorge provided a sharp reminder of just how small man really was in comparison to the vastness of nature. The current slowed as they neared the deep water of the hydro dam's head pond. Paddling to the shore, once there they dragged the canoes up onto the bank and loaded up for the portage around the man-made barrier. Back on the water below the dam, they were paddling along when Joseph told Nick that he had been accepted into the University of Alaska at Fairbanks.

"Great. Are you sticking with business or trying something else?"

"Sociology," came the reply. Joseph stopped paddling, turning to look back at Nick. "I want to work with kids — Native kids as much as possible."

"That's pretty commendable." Nick stopped paddling too and their canoe drifted lazily along. "You and your family have been blessed, Joseph. Giving something back is the best thing I could ever hope for from you."

The following morning when Joseph woke up, the wind had died down and turned in their favour. He slipped quietly from the tent, went for a swim, then made a fire and prepared tea, all before five o'clock. Soon, everyone else was out and around, walking down to the lakeshore to wash up. No one else had Joseph's courage to jump into the frigid waters of the lake.

Leah helped Tom prepare breakfast while Joseph and Nick packed up the tents and their gear, and reloaded the canoes. Invigorated by the beautiful weather, within a few hours they crossed the Lake and were back on the River. That day, with a slight wind at their backs and a strong current, they were able to travel fifty-five miles to a place called Big Salmon. The next day they passed through Little Salmon and camped on the banks of the Yukon River.

At ten o'clock in the morning of the fifth day they pulled into Carmacks. Leah could hardly wait to show Tom the place where she had been born. When they reached the house she was disappointed and slightly embarrassed. The tidy little bungalow her grandparents had built, and the place where her mother, her brother and she herself had been born, was now abandoned. With its windows broken, and a roof caved in from the weight of unshoveled snow, the once lively home sat forlorn, lost forever through time and neglect. Within the crumbling walls of the house that meant so much to them, now only the packrats that scurried about, called the place home.

Taking Tom by the hand, a distressed Leah walked back to the canoes. Joseph too turned away and followed his sister from the terrible sight.

An hour downriver, the subdued group approached Five Finger Rapids. Pulling into shore, they donned their life jackets and tied down all the supplies. Slipping back into the water, they paddled towards the growing sound of roaring rapids. Almost

147

without warning, the river, swollen by the heavy winter snowfall and a late spring runoff, quickly erupted into a watery turmoil.

Behind Leah and Tom, a genuinely concerned Nick watched as their canoe nosed into the second set of churning rapids. Then, the unthinkable happened when Tom lost his paddle and made the mistake of leaning out too far in an attempt to retrieve it. As soon as he did, the canoe tipped dangerously and Leah hollered: "Tom! Forget the paddle — lean into the curl." But it was too late, and in a split second, the canoe flipped over.

Nick and Joseph dug their paddles deep, straining to move forward as fast as possible while maintaining their balance in the surging waters. Leah's head popped to the surface and she instantly began treading water, eyes searching as she struggled against the whirlpool that had swallowed Tom and the canoe.

Nick and Joseph maneuvered their canoe to an eddy just above the whirlpool. "I'm going in," Joseph shouted above the deafening roar. Nick hesitated, and then nodded, his eyes darting back and forth between the boy's sister, and the swirling recess into which Tom had disappeared. Steadying the canoe, Nick watched as Joseph stood up, glanced skywards, made a small gesture, then dove into the middle of the whirlpool.

Nick's arms gripped the paddle, keeping the canoe steady, ready to move. His eyes scoured the surface for Leah in time to see her being carried downstream. His mind screamed for him to dive in after her but he fought that dangerous instinct. Certain that almost two minutes had passed since Tom went under, all he could do was wait for Joseph to reappear. Torn between the emptiness in front of him, and the girl being pulled through the rapids, a tormented Nick Roberts waited in near frantic desperation. All of a sudden, Joseph reappeared just below the whirlpool — in the grip of one arm he held Tom around the neck.

Joseph flipped on his back and, kicking his feet in the water, began hauling Tom's limp body towards the shore. Instantly Nick glanced downriver, then looked back at Joseph, pointing his free arm. Nick dug his paddle deep and the canoe shot forward over the whirlpool.

An exhausted Leah reached out to grab hold of the protruding edge of a basalt rock. Nick shouted that he was coming but his words fell on deaf ears as she slipped underwater. As his canoe

Joseph diving into the whirlpool.

raced towards the spot where she had been, behind him, an exhausted Joseph reached the bank where he struggled to pull Tom onto the shore.

Nick's eyes searched the water and as he was about to dive in when Leah's head floated to the surface. He pushed hard on the paddle and in near desperation reached out to grab her by the hair and lifted her head out of the water. The canoe tilted and he struggled to hold her while fighting through the last giant curl of the rapids. With one final push from the powerful current, the front of the canoe dove under the water, surfaced, then settled quietly, half full of water, in the calm near the shore. Leah gagged and Nick's mind screamed with joy at the sound. Turning to look far upstream, he could see Joseph working to resuscitate Tom and as the boy glanced up, Nick waved a happy signal that he and Leah were okay.

On shore, a frightened Leah asked Nick if Tom had made it through the rapids. Nick pointed upstream to where a revived Tom was now sitting up. Just below where they were sitting, the other canoe had come to a halt on a sandbar. Nick waded out and pulled the battered canoe to shore. Tom and Leah's sleeping bags were still stuffed under the seats but the tent and all the supplies were gone. Worse though, the canvas had been punctured at the waterline and before they could go anywhere, it would have to be repaired.

Nick emptied the water from the other canoe and unloaded its drenched contents. After securing both canoes high on the shore he walked up the embankment and collected bits of dry driftwood and grass. He dug into one of the waterlogged knapsacks and pulled out the metal cylinder containing the waterproof matches. As soon as he had a strong fire burning, he hugged Leah and told her to rest while he went back to help Joseph and Tom.

Nick picked his way along the difficult rocky shoreline to where the two young men were sitting. "How's Leah?" they both asked in unison.

After he reassured them she was fine, and waved back at her, Tom said he was anxious to get back to Leah.

"You sure you're up to it? We can rest here for a while longer," Nick said. But a nervous Tom insisted on going immediately.

Leah looked up from the fire as the three men came into site. Dropping the things in her hands, she ran and hugged Tom, then turned and held her brother close.

"I'm sorry Leah, this is my fault. I should have checked on the rapids before we came," Joseph said, almost in tears.

"Forget it, it was an accident," she kissed his cheek and Tom, who stood there a little lost, watched as the young girl took charge. She already had their gear spread out to dry in the sun near the fire, and was in the process of preparing the materials to repair the holes in the damaged canoe.

With almost half of their supplies lost to the river, they would have to ration the food for the rest of the trip. Nonetheless, Leah insisted they eat a solid meal.

By four o'clock in the afternoon most of their things had dried in the warm summer sun and Leah had patched the holes in the canoe. Reloaded with what remaining gear they had, the foursome slipped their canoes back into the river.

After the trauma they had been through, that night they decided to stay at a public campground along the river and were pleased they were able to buy a small amount of canned food and a few chocolate bars.

Just past noon on the sixth day they arrived at Fort Selkirk where they set up camp on a sandbar. They were eating lunch and watching a pair of ducks swimming by when suddenly Joseph slipped into the river and silently dove under water. The next thing they noticed was one of the ducks going under the water, feet first. A moment later, the other one disappeared.

The shocked trio on shore watched as Joseph came up, waving the two ducks in his hand. His face beaming as he emerged from the water, Joseph said: "Tonight we dine compliments of Mother Nature, with a little help from the Great Spirit."

Tom watched in stunned silence, Leah smiled and an amazed Nick asked where Joseph had learned to do that.

"Your Métis buddy, Jerry Beaumont!" the boy grinned.

They used the rest of the day to explore the ghost town of Fort Selkirk. That evening, Joseph roasted the ducks over an open fire, made bannock, cattail shoots, wild onions, and Labrador tea. Later, as they sat around the fire singing songs, suddenly Nick and then Joseph noticed the shadowy image moving along the ridge several hundred feet up the mountain.

"Are you thinking what I'm thinking?" They looked at each other.

"You bet," Joseph replied. "Let's hope he keeps going."

A large grizzly made its way along the summit to a position downwind from where they were camped. Every once in a while the big grizzly stopped, stood on its hind legs, sniffed the air, and let out a grunt. After a few minutes, it turned and appeared to be headed directly towards them.

Nick and Joseph jumped to their feet. "We're getting out of here," Nick said. "Take down the camp and load up, but be ready to drop everything and get in your canoe.

Safely on the water, they stopped paddling and waited, watching their spot on the riverbank. Sure enough, the grizzly appeared exactly where their campsite had been. Leah's friend Tom nervously stared across the water at the bear, his face turning a ghostly white when the giant grizzly stood on its hind legs, opened its huge jaws wide, and let out a tremendous roar.

From the bow of their canoe, Leah turned to look back at Nick and a wide smile came to both of their faces. Joseph looked over from his canoe and knew exactly what they were thinking. "Tom," he said digging the paddle deep into the water. "Ask Leah to tell you about the day we looked a giant grizzly straight in the eye!"

Making certain they got plenty far away from the grizzly, they paddled for most of the night, taking advantage of the Yukon's 24-hour sunshine. By early morning, exhausted and needing warm food and a good sleep, they felt it was safe enough to make camp. Nevertheless, they did so, on the opposite side of the river.

Rested, they set out again in the afternoon, canoeing until late evening when they stopped to camp at Stewart River. Ahead of schedule, they pulled into Dawson City one day before Miranda and Dan were to arrive.

They booked rooms at a local hotel, took a good shower, and ate a wonderful meal. After a good night of sleep, they met for coffee then explored the city for a little while before returning to the dock to wait for their vehicles.

When Dan and Miranda drove up, Tom turned to Leah and said: "Do you think we should tell your mom about what happened at the rapids?"

Leah glanced over at Nick who shook his head, yes. Turning to look at her boyfriend, in a voice loud enough to ensure Nick got the message, she said: "What rapids?"

CHAPTER 22

Return to the Yukon River

A T AN AGE WHEN MOST PEOPLE were thinking about retirement or at least slowing down, Nick Roberts was making plans to climb to the top of Mt. McKinley. Joseph however, had ideas of his own, wanting Nick to canoe the remainder of the Yukon River with him. Of course Joseph was more important than any mountain and so over the winter their telephone calls centered on a canoeing expedition from where they had left off the year before at Dawson City, all the way down to where the river emptied into the Bering Sea.

Joseph calculated that they should be able to cover that distance in about seventeen to eighteen days. That was a too much all at once and as such they decided on eight days that coming summer, limiting the trip to the approximate seven hundred miles between Dawson City and the E. L. Patton Bridge crossing the James Dalton Highway in Alaska. The following year they could return to the bridge and continue with an equally long journey all the way through the state of Alaska to the Bering Sea.

This time when Nick stepped off the plane, the neatly dressed young gentleman waiting for him brought home the reality that time was marching on.

Again this year, Dan and Miranda offered to drop them off at their starting point but Leah insisted she and Tom be the ones to pick them up at the bridge eight days later.

They left the dock at Dawson City in Joseph's new seventeen-foot freighter canoe, loaded down with enough food and supplies to last for a little more than ten days. Their trip, although quiet, even dull in comparison to prior adventures, turned out to be one of their best. As they paddled under glorious blue skies for eight perfect days, Joseph talked a lot about his hopes and dreams for the future. When they reached the bridge on the James Dalton

Highway where Tom and Leah were waiting, both of them wished they could keep paddling, all the way to the Bering Sea.

That winter, for the first time ever, Nick Roberts spent Christmas with his adopted family. The invitation to do something that had never crossed his mind before, came from out of the blue.

"Nick," Miranda reminded him, "it was sixteen years ago when we shared Christmas in the tepee. It's time we do it again. Besides," she paused, "we may never get another chance — I'm about to lose my baby."

On the other end of the line, Nick Roberts' confused mind tried to grasp her meaning.

"Leah is getting married," she said.

Nick carried the portable phone to his apartment living-room and sat down in the armchair. "Congratulations, I guess. I mean well — I don't know what I mean." Nick's mind was still trying to comprehend the reality.

Miranda laughed. "She and Tom have tentatively set July 3rd, if that works out for you. Anyway, we can discuss it at Christmas. You will come, won't you?"

"I'd love to Miranda, I really would."

Nick pestered more sales clerks than any man in Vancouver, but in the end, he found exactly the Christmas gifts he wanted to deliver in person. Keeping with the spirit of the holidays, even the check-in girl at the airport counter said nothing when the smiling man showed up with a pushcart overflowing with heavy boxes.

During his Christmas visit, Joseph came home from university, making the trip by air from Fairbanks to Whitehorse. They all spent a great deal of time talking about Leah's wedding plans. Tom's parents came by for dinner and another night they all went out to a restaurant together.

To Nick's pleasant surprise, Leah asked him to give her away. Dan had been a loving and devoted stepfather to the children and Leah would never dream of hurting his feelings. So, long before Christmas, she asked her mom if she thought Dan would feel slighted were she to ask Nick. Miranda told her that he had kind of expected it, and was in full agreement.

Although Nick would never say a word, he felt Leah was a bit young to commit to marriage. On the other hand, he knew part of it was his not wanting to let go. However, the brilliant girl would graduate from university in the spring, getting a degree in sylviculture before her 21st birthday. Her chosen field was a natural for someone like Leah and she had already been offered a job with the Yukon government that would allow her to work in the Whitehorse area.

Nick returned in late spring to be there for her graduation but had to fly back to Vancouver immediately. When he arrived the afternoon before her wedding, Leah, Miranda, and Melissa, were busy decorating the hall and getting the flowers ready. Joseph rushed him over to a rehearsal and afterwards, when the women said they had a million things still to do, Nick offered to take Joseph, Tom and Tom's father out for dinner. "Sure, but how about him?" Joseph whispered looking over Nick's shoulder at the church's front door.

A puzzled expression covered Nick's face and he turned to look where Joseph was staring. In the doorway, the unmistakable image of Jerry Beaumont loomed large.

The wedding ceremony was a beautiful event, with Joseph as best man and Tom's older sister the matron of honor. The small church was filled to capacity when Nick stepped out of the limousine in a black tuxedo, a red carnation in his lapel, and a red hankie in the breast pocket. He turned and helped Leah from the car. The photographer's camera flashed several times, catching the striking image of the young lady in the long white gown. Beneath the white veil, happy dark eyes flashed at Nick as she took him by the arm.

The moment they entered the vestibule, the wedding march began playing and the rustling sound of people turning all at once to stare soon changed to oohs and aahs as Leah and Nick made their entrance. Halfway down the aisle, a nervous and self-conscious Nick almost tripped over the carpet but it was the calm and collected Leah who gripped him tight and kept moving on. As they approached the altar and Tom turned to look at his future bride, a tear welled-up in the corner of Nick's eye and he fought desperately not to cry.

The waiting groom, dressed in a black tux, fidgeted with his fingers and swallowed hard, trying to stop from shaking. Joseph, dressed the same as Nick, appeared as calm as could be until Nick noticed the sweat pouring from the edge of his brow.

When the ceremony was over, the bride and groom left in the limousine, making their entrance at the reception hall after their guests had all arrived. At the head table they were flanked by the wedding party and their family, including Nick.

A local band provided the music for dancing and Tom politely led off the ceremonial first dance with his new mother-in-law. As Nick watched Joseph and the lovely young lady he was currently dating, from the way she seemed to cling to his every word, he felt certain there would be another wedding to attend before long.

Leah and Tom left the hall shortly after midnight, while their guests celebrated into the wee hours of the morning.

On the Monday following the wedding, Nick and Joseph drove to Skagway on the Alaskan panhandle. Joseph had a friend in Juneau who owned his own fishing boat. For years, he had been asking Joseph to come out fishing with him. Somehow things always came up and Joseph had been too busy, until now.

Hubert Longfoot was readying his forty-two-foot fishing trawler when Joseph and Nick showed up at the wharf. Clean and well maintained, the old trawler had surprisingly large bunkrooms and a sizeable galley with refrigerator, cooking range, and microwave oven.

An hour after they left the Skagway wharf, they pulled into the docks at Haines where Hubert had a brief but important meeting. As soon as he was done, they stocked up with food and topped off the fuel tanks for the voyage south down the Chatham Straits. By six o'clock in the evening they were anchored in the narrow bay in Icy Strait.

Before starting supper, their host baited a crab trap with frozen herring and threw it overboard. By the time Hubert had the potatoes and carrots peeled, an amazed Nick helped pull up a crab trap so full they could hardly lift it into the boat. After picking out six big ones for their dinner, they released the rest back into the bay.

Nick set the table and Joseph made a salad while Hubert cooked the crabs. As a special treat for his guests, he prepared them in a variety of ways. Some were baked with garlic, some with mushrooms, and some sautéed with onions and bacon. It was, without question, the best crab Nick and Joseph had never tasted.

Although the day had been clear under a warm sun, by the time they pulled anchor and got under way a damp breeze moved in, whipping a chill across the strait. They traveled west for almost an hour before heading north into Glacier Bay. Nick and Joseph drank hot coffee and watched the spectacular scenery slide by. Sheer cliffs of ice dropped into the sea with such a tremendous thunder that it could be heard for miles. Around them, tourists lined the rails of the huge cruise ships moving slowly around the bay.

They fished all next day in calm seas, but on the way home a storm came up and Hubert asked them to pitch in and tie down everything on the deck. There had nicely finished and had stepped into the wheelhouse when a huge wave almost swamped the boat. For an inexperienced Joseph and Nick it was a terrifying experience as their minds told them that they were going down. For Hubert, it was just another thing that came with the job he loved.

The trip was a marvelous adventure, but safely back at Skagway, Nick seriously considered kissing the dock

CHAPTER 23

The Yukon River to the Sea

L EAH AND TOM HONEYMOONED in Hawaii, spending ten days in Maui where they visited Puaa Kaa State Park. Neither had ever been to any place tropical before and it was especially enjoyable for Leah to experience the island's lush vegetation and to visit the park's magnificent waterfalls and its sparkling mountain pools, all things that presented a sharp contrast to the vast tundra of her native Yukon.

Their flight home connected through Vancouver, and the honeymooners spent three days with Nick. He delighted in showing them the city, visiting the Aquarium at Stanley Park, the Vancouver Museum, and the Granville Island Market. But for two young people who had spent their lives in a small town in the northern wilderness, the city's nightlife was an irresistible attraction. Nick left them to see that part of the city on their own.

Over the ensuing winter, Joseph and Nick agreed that for the next summer they would complete the last leg of their canoe trip down the Yukon River that would take them to the Bering Sea. After studying the route carefully, Joseph phoned to say that he felt they should allow eleven days to complete the voyage instead of the nine he had originally calculated.

"I have four friends from university who would like to join us. Do you mind?"

"Not at all, if you think they can handle it" Nick replied. "Will Leah and Tom be coming?"

A disappointed Nick listened as Joseph said: "Unfortunately they can't coordinate their vacation schedules."

It was a lot easier for Nick to fly in and out of the airport at Fairbanks but by meeting Joseph and the others in the Alaskan city instead of in Whitehorse, it meant he would not see Miranda or

Leah this trip. However, his own schedule this year was tight and it was a long trip they were undertaking. Under the circumstances, he felt he had little choice but to take a non-stop jet from Seattle.

On his arrival at the Fairbanks airport, Joseph, with one of his friends, was there to pick him up. After their usual routine of hugs and patting each other on the back, Joseph introduced him to his fellow student, Victor Mallory.

"Pleased to meet you, Victor," Nick looked around. "Joseph? Where's the rest of our group?"

"They're all so gung-ho, they're already up at the bridge loading the supplies into the canoes."

A broad grin came and Nick said: "In that case, wait here — I won't be long." He picked up one of his suitcases and headed to the men's room. A few minutes later he strode back, dressed in his waterproof outdoor clothing and steel-toed boots.

"I'm sorry, Nick." Joseph laughed. "I was so excited too, that I never thought about you needing to change."

Nick wasn't about to admit to his own excitement. No matter how many trips he made, every time he traveled north his heart started racing long before the plane even landed. "So, how did you get all the gear up here?" he asked, giving Joseph his patented rub on the head.

"No problem. Two of the guy's have vans so we hauled everything in them with the canoes strapped on top. Victor and I brought the vans here because it's a lot safer leaving them in the airport parking lot. We hired a local guy to drive us up."

"Let me take those, Mr. Roberts," Victor said, picking up Nick's bags.

"Thanks — and it's just plain Nick."

"Yes sir, Nick."

"Where are you from, Victor?" Nick asked, unsure of the heavy foreign accent.

"South Africa — Cape Town, sir."

"Beautiful country."

"Have you been there, Mr. ah, Nick?"

"Just once, years ago. Quite an experience, canoeing the Berg River."

"Really," the young man said, admiration written across his face.

159

When their driver dropped them at the river, Joseph's three young friends had everything loaded and were sitting in their canoes under the long bridge. Paddles in hand, they were ready to shove off.

Joseph pointed to each one, introducing Nick to Eric Philips from Queensland, Australia, Bender Singh from India, and Albert Beaulieu, a Dogrib Indian from Yellowknife, in Canada's Northwest Territories.

Suddenly Joseph stopped, looked at Nick then all his friends. "Now, this is really a United Nations expedition," he laughed.

They excited young men waited for Nick to load his personal things into his canoe before pushing off. Their long voyage began with boyish yells, whoops, and splashing of each other with their paddles as they headed down stream. Nick groaned — to himself.

Joseph joined Ben in the lead canoe, followed by Albert and Eric, with Nick and Victor bringing up the rear. Because of the more than seven hundred miles of river between them and the Bering Sea, everyone wore gloves, not wanting to take the chance of getting blisters that could make it impossible to paddle.

They traveled steadily, only stopping long enough to cook dinner, then they were back in the canoes and continuing downstream. Just after midnight, when the sun had dipped behind the mountain peeks, they tied the three canoes together and took turns staying awake to keep them floating down the center of the river.

For the next couple of days the sky stayed clear and the weather warm with only a slight northwesterly breeze. Their paddling took them past large herds of caribou grazing on the tundra, an Arctic fox running back and forth along the bank looking for mice, and a cow moose leading her twin calves away from danger.

Just before the Village of Nulato, the river turned and headed almost straight south. The tundra disappeared behind Kaiyug Mountain, and the lush grasslands turned into tall lodge-pole pines.

Just as suddenly as the landscape changed, so did the weather. The blue sky turned overcast and ominous storm clouds blew in with the wind from the south.

They had just pulled over to a sandbar to put on their rain gear when the first downpour hit. Rushing to get covered up, they dressed and jumped back into their canoes, the rain stinging their faces as they paddled into an ever-increasing wind. The river was wide at that point and as the wind swept across it, the surface turned choppy.

By six o'clock that evening it was a cold and wet group that pulled into shore. Shivering, they rushed to set up their tents then Joseph got a large fire going and Nick began preparing dinner. After the others had changed into dry clothes, they hung a heavy piece of plastic sheeting between the tent and the fire to protect them from the rain. Two of them put their rain gear back on and set about to gather enough wood to keep the fire going all night.

Within half an hour, the dry clothes, roaring fire and the smell of a good meal cooking, changed the quiet mood. "This is grizzly country, and they have a powerful sense of smell," Joseph warned his friends. "After we eat, we're going to have to store the food at least a quarter of a mile away from the camp." As he spoke, Nick appeared from the tent with his rifle in hand.

"We learned one tough lesson from a hungry grizzly, and that was enough," Nick said placing his rifle under the plastic, safely out of the rain.

Nick had been standing over the pot of boiling stew for less than five minutes when he heard the loud crash in the bush. He looked over to where the sound came from and saw Eric Philips bending down to pick up wood for the fire. Behind him, in an all too familiar frightening scene, a large grizzly sped to the attack.

In the few seconds it took Nick to grab his rifle, inject a shell into the chamber, and fire, the bear was already within a few yards of Eric. When Nick fired, the shot hit the animal in the shoulder and the giant bear let out a bellow. Veering in the direction of the sound of the gunfire, it spotted Nick. Understanding Nick was the danger, the wounded bear, foaming angrily at the mouth, let out a savage roar and charged directly towards him.

Nick fired a second shot into the bear's chest, stepped aside, and fired once more. The bear landed with a huge thud in the exact spot where Nick had been standing.

A dazed Eric Philips stumbled over to where Joseph stood by the fire. Trembling with fear from his brush with sure death, the young man sat down on the ground, and trembled.

Bender Singh, who had witnessed it all, stood on the rock precipice, his arms filled with bits of firewood, unable to move.

"Joseph, go get your friend Bender."

"What's up with the gunfire, guys?" an almost casual Albert Beaulieu asked as he emerged from his tent. All at once he stopped in his tracks, staring down at the huge grizzly bear lying on the ground in front of him. "Holy cow!" he said, looking around, checking to see if anyone had been hurt.

"Albert, why don't you go bring Eric out of the rain. Maybe sit with him for a while. He's pretty shook up. The bear was attacking him when I shot it."

"Holy cow!" Albert repeated his words, running to comfort his frightened friend.

Looking down at the dead bear, he felt no pride nor pleasure in killing such a magnificent creature. He had only a feeling of guilt and sadness for having done what he did. He knew that if he hadn't made that split second decision to shoot, the grizzly would have killed one or maybe all of them. This was an unprovoked attack and there was nothing they could have done differently that would have prevented it. The bear was old and no doubt happened to be in a bad mood at the time.

Joseph and Albert skinned the bear and after storing the hide in the canoe, they rolled the carcass down the bank and into the river so it wouldn't attract any more bears to the area. Nick kept talking as he took over the preparation of their dinner. Occupying their thoughts with other things helped a little but when their meal was ready, no one was hungry and they only toyed with their food.

Gratefully, the hard rain turned to a drizzle and finally stopped altogether. Nick and Joseph gathered more wood, this time Nick carried the rifle and the two never strayed far from one another. No one got much sleep that night; there was usually two or three of the boys sitting around the fire, holding the loaded rifle, and staring into the bush. Although Joseph had warned his friends about the possibility of a grizzly encounter, not even he had expected an attack such as this.

Although the rains returned by morning, after eating breakfast everyone was anxious to get into the canoes and away from the scene. When they got to the middle of the river, there was a definite feeling of relief amongst all the young men.

By about noon the rain stopped, this time for good. The wind died down and the sun began to warm the landscape. The weather changed their mood and the easy banter, although far less than at the beginning of their trip, returned.

They stopped at the edge of the village of Kaltag where they lit a fire on the bank to dry themselves off. When they were warm and dry, Nick and Joseph went into the village to find someone who could use the bear hide. With the warm weather, it would have to be tanned as soon as possible or it would quickly spoil.

In the village they were directed to an old Indian woman who lived another two miles down river. They were told that she was the only one left in the community that could still tans hides the old way. Back in their canoes, they set off to find the woman's home. Within half an hour they spotted a large white tepee set in a clearing beside the river. When they got closer they could see several hides hanging over smudge fires. They knew they were at the right place.

Albert Beaulieu, the Dogrib Indian familiar with native traditions, led the way up the narrow trail to the clearing with Eric Philips on his heels. Soon everyone else hopped out of their canoes and scampered up after them. "Greetings," Albert called out as they approached the old lady sitting in front of her tepee, working a hide.

She glanced up at the boys, waved an arm across her face, and said, "Honeene."

Albert greeted her in his native tongue, then turned and asked Joseph if he understood what she was saying.

"Just a little," Joseph told him. "I think she wants to know who we are and what we want."

"Good, that's what I thought, too."

Joseph and Albert stumbled through a few words with the elderly woman. Between them, they managed to learn her name was Ada Ongtooguk and that she had lived on this spot her entire life.

"Can you ask her if she wants the bear skin," Nick spoke up.

After more struggled conversation between the old woman and the boys, Albert said, "I'm pretty sure what she wants is to check it first."

When they placed the hide at her feet she picked up one edge and began a meticulous examination. Finally, in her native tongue, she told the boys she would do the job but it would take three weeks.

"No," Nick said when they told him. "Explain to her that the hide is a gift."

As Albert spoke, Nick saw the old woman's face light up, her head nodding in gratitude. Touched by the simplicity, he went down to his canoe on the shore where he rifled through one of his packs until he found what he wanted. Returning to the tepee, Nick reached into his pocket and handed the old woman a pouch. The toothless smile broadened when she saw what it was. Immediately she removed an object from her dress pocket, tapped in some of the tobacco with her thumb, and with a relishing smile, lit the pipe. Puffing away, she reached back into the pouch, taking out a pinch of tobacco between gnarled fingers. Her head nodded to them again and her arm reached out. Fingers opened, letting bits of tobacco float away on the breeze.

"How did you know she smoked? And how come she threw some of the tobacco away?" one of the boys asked.

"I didn't," Nick said. "But a number of the natives along the river use tobacco for some of their offerings so I brought a small pouch for goodwill in case we needed to ask a favor."

"Offerings? What's that?" the Australian, Eric Philips wanted to know.

"If the natives catch a lot of fish in one area, they might sprinkle a little tobacco on the water. Or, if they shoot a caribou, or in this case when strangers come bearing a gift from nature, they would toss some tobacco into the wind. It's a symbol, their way of giving something back."

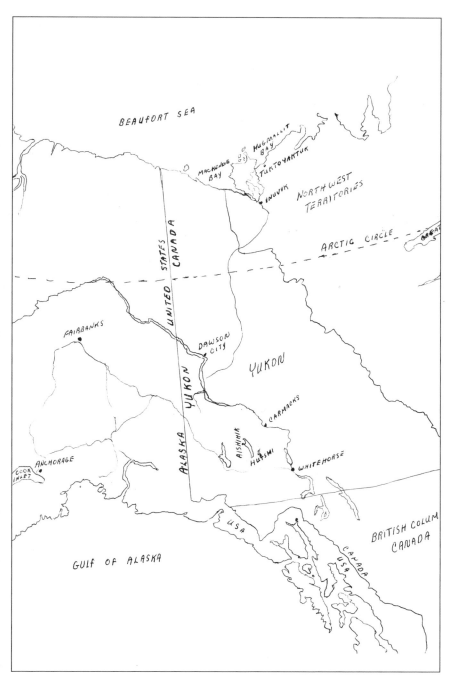

CHAPTER 24

The Chilkoot Trail

AFTER THEIR TRIP down the Yukon River to the Bering Sea, Joseph and Nick discussed a change in venue for the next year to a hike of the Chilkoot Trail. An old Indian route, used by the gold seekers at the end of the 19th century, they could follow the trail from Skagway, Alaska, through the mountains to the headwaters of the Yukon River at Bennett Lake. Although they wouldn't be doing it, from Bennett Lake it was possible to canoe down the Yukon River to the Klondike gold fields at Dawson City. Joseph said he had read that over eighty thousand people started out in the search for gold, but fewer than thirty thousand actually made it all the way to Dawson City. "The book says that the remnants of those times are still very evident along the trail."

"Sounds good. Maybe I'll read up a little on it, too." Nick told him.

Joseph planned on making the thirty-five-mile trip from Skagway to Bennett Lake in five days. He told Nick they could probably do it in three days if they hiked straight through, but five days gave them time to make a few side trips.

This time, Leah, Tom, Dan, Miranda, and Melissa were all coming along. It would be the first time they had all taken a trip together since the Mackenzie Delta trip more than a dozen years before.

Joseph spent months preparing for the trip and had everything ready. The first night they would stay at the campground in Dyea, Alaska, followed by four nights in the mountains. He marked each spot on the map he sent Nick showing where they would camp overnight as well as the two side trips that were planned from places called Canyon City and Happy Camp.

On the day of their departure, Joseph had divided all the supplies into seven backpacks and knew exactly what each person would be carrying. The packs would be heavy due to the need for a variety of clothing as a result of the possibility of severe changes in weather conditions at that time of year. He explained that at the high altitude they needed to climb to in order to cross the mountains, they could expect heat, cold, rain, snow, fog, or any combination.

"There is a stretch that runs for about seventeen miles between Sheep Camp, and Deep Lake," Joseph said, pointing at his map. "There, we can expect rapidly changing weather and winds in excess of fifty miles an hour."

Miranda looked at him. "And you want me to go there? Are you crazy?"

"Yup," Joseph smiled and hugged his mother who shrugged her shoulders at Nick.

On the way to Skagway, they stopped at Bennett Lake to drop off one of the vehicles to be used at the end of their trip. From there, everyone squeezed into Nick's new SUV and they arrived in Skagway in time for lunch at a local saloon. After their meal, they toured the town for a couple of hours before setting up their tents at the Dyea campground.

That evening they explored the area around their campsite in Dyea They found very little remains of the town except for an old graveyard. Another visitor said that an employee of the National Park Service told her that the cemetery was where victims of the 1898 Palm Sunday avalanche had been buried. She told them that no one knew for certain how many people were killed or who all was buried there because of the discrepancies in the newspaper accounts of the day but that it ranged from 60 to 100 victims.

In the morning they had everything packed and were on the trail early. The first part was swampy, with a gradual climb through a rain forest of tall fir, spruce, and lodge-pole pines. They followed the well-marked narrowing trail past an old sawmill then stopped for lunch beside the Taiya River at a place called Finnegan's Point.

Acting like a professional guide, Joseph had brought a notepad with all kinds of information written down. As they walked or when they stopped to eat, he explained the history and the various points of interest. According to Joseph's information, Finnegan's Point was one of the places the gold seekers used to rally their supplies from one cache up to the next. Everyone heading for the

Klondike gold fields had to bring at least a thousand pounds of food to make sure they had enough to sustain them for one year. At that time, Dawson City was not established enough to support the tens of thousands of people gripped by gold fever who were flocking to the town. It took an average of three months and dozens of trips back and forth carrying their supplies to get through the mountains. Once they got all their supplies to Bennett Lake, they built boats and floated down the Yukon River to Dawson City.

"Unfortunately," Joseph shook his head, smiling as they began walking again. "After all that work, by the time most of them got there, every claim in the Klondike had already been staked."

By five o'clock that afternoon they had reached Canyon City. Miranda, Leah, and Melissa set up the tents, while Nick, Dan, Tom, and Joseph prepared dinner. The girls slept in the small tent and the guys slept in the larger one. Due to the dry conditions on the mountain, fire restrictions were in force and no open fires were permitted.

The next day they crossed the suspension bridge over the Taiya River to the ruins of another of the old towns that had sprung up during the gold rush days. There was very little evidence that a town had actually existed or that it had over a thousand inhabitants at one time. All they saw were a few old bottles, a couple of tin cans, and what looked like part of a rusted-out washtub. "Everything along this trail, including those rusty old tin cans are protected by law," Joseph said. "There are pretty hefty fines for anyone caught removing or destroying them."

The trail between Canyon City and Pleasant Camp started getting steeper and steeper. By the time they got to the spot called Sheep Camp, they began running into patches of snow and ice. But here, above the tree line, they could see the country below them for miles. They stopped for lunch at the bottom of the steepest part of the trail in a place Joseph's notes said was called the Scales. Ahead was a forty-five degree climb to the summit of the mountain at the thirty-four-hundred-foot level. This part of the trail, known as the "Golden Stairs," had been carved out of the sharp rocks. With the weather they were having, it was very wet and slippery.

At the top of the Golden Stairs was a sign that read Canada-U.S. Border, Welcome to Canada. When they finally reached Stone Crib, at the foot of Crater Lake, they could see down the other side of the mountain. The steepest climb was behind them but still ahead was a rapid descent down the mountain's winding, rocky trail. To almost everyone's surprise, they found that going down was almost as hard as climbing up.

By six-thirty that evening they reached Happy Camp, so called because when hikers arrived there, they all felt relieved that the hardest part of the trail was behind them. It was the first time in his life that Nick felt the strain from any arduous activity.

They were all eager for a hot meal and Happy Camp was one of the spots along the way where campfires were permitted. Leah and Melissa insisted on making dinner while everyone else rested. It was a little after ten o'clock when their tents were all set up and everyone was ready for bed.

The weather had remained warm and sunny throughout the trip and when they went to bed the sun was still shining. Happy Camp was on a plateau with three small lakes nearby. The plateau was covered with a variety of vegetation, from heather and grasses to small clumps of willows covered with tiny yellow flowers.

The lakes were clear emerald green with a mirrored surface that reflected the mountains high above them. The water in the lakes was so cold that your teeth would sting when you drank it. The air was very clean and fresh with the smell of flowers and a hint of pine that Miranda said made her wish she could bottle it to take home.

The place was so spectacular that they did nothing but play all day, climbing the hills and sliding down on the mountainside heather. Joseph and Dan went up to one of the lakes and came back with a supply of fish for an excellent large supper.

In the morning everyone was up early, packing the tents and preparing for the final leg of the trip. Tom fried pans full of bacon and eggs while Joseph made tea and a large pan of golden bannock. As they set around eating, there was so much they wanted to talk about but no one said anything. Instead, they thought of times past, understanding that this would be the last day they would all spend together, and probably the last time for a long while.

It was almost nine o'clock by the time they got on the trail. The last part of the trip was probably the most beautiful. The trail to Bennett Lake gradually descended into a fir and pine forest that surrounded their final destination.

CHAPTER 25

Natalie

NICK ROBERTS HAD BEEN THRILLED when Leah called to tell him she was expecting her first child. His excitement grew even more when she phoned to say it would be twins. But when he visited her home and held her baby girls in his arms for the first time, a feeling came unlike anything he'd ever known possible.

Leah had gone through a rough time. Once out of the hospital and at home, she still had to spend a full week in bed. A thoughtful Tom took time off work to help take care of her and the twins. Tom cooked, washed dishes, cleaned, did the vacuuming, and when anyone showed up for a visit, bragged endlessly about his daughters.

Chelsea and Brittany, as they had been christened, quickly became the focal point of their proud grandmother's life. Miranda doted on them, telling Leah that the joy of being a grandmother meant she could totally spoil the children then leave her and Tom with the problem.

Joseph had spent at least one week with Nick every summer over the past seventeen years, but that year when Leah gave birth, Joseph wouldn't tell Nick where they were going. He told him it was a surprise and he would find out when he got to Whitehorse. Nick knew that no matter where, as long as he and Joseph were together, he would enjoy the time.

Nick supposed it had something to do with his new job so when Joseph met him at the airport with a beautiful young lady at his side, he was pretty sure it wasn't work related. He was wrong.

The petite girl Joseph introduced as Natalie had dazzling dark eyes that captivated Nick the moment he saw her. From the way Joseph looked at her, Nick had no doubt the boy was totally in love.

"Hello, Natalie. It's a pleasure to meet you. Is this the surprise you told me about?" Nick smiled, holding out his arms to greet her.

"One of the surprises!" Joseph said. "There's another one, too. We wondered if this year you might like to join us on a special camping trip? We are taking a group of underprivileged kids to visit one of communities just across the Yukon border in British Columbia."

"Joseph told me you're a great teller of old Indian legends," Natalie interjected. "I hope you will let me convince you to come along with us."

"No convincing needed," Nick said. "I'd love to go."

"That's what Joseph said you would say," Natalie smiled.

As they drove home, Natalie told Nick she was also a social worker, who specialized in dealing with troubled children. "We met when we were both working at some of the communities along the Alaska-Yukon border."

"Luckiest day of his life," Nick quipped and Joseph blushed.

That evening, in Joseph's apartment, he learned that Natalie had been born in the little village of Katovik, on the Beaufort Sea. After returning from World War II, her grandfather bought a caterpillar tractor and several covered sleds from the United States government. The surplus equipment, left over after construction of the Alaska Highway, allowed her grandfather, and eventually her father, to improve and expand the business. Before the modern machinery, her grandfather's opportunities were limited because the only transport available was by dogsled. With the tractor he traveled about buying such things as Arctic char from the Indians and Eskimos and trading them for nets and other supplies.

Natalie told Nick that she had attended school in Fairbanks and after high school went on to university, graduating with a degree in sociology. While still a small girl, she had been deeply troubled by the emotional problems many of the native families were having as a result of the rapid changes taking place in their lives. At a young age, Natalie had made up her mind to do something about it. And now, in Joseph, she had met someone who shared her vision.

"We first met at Old Crow, a small village on the Porcupine River in the northwest corner of the Yukon Territories," she told

Nick while Joseph sat next to her, holding her hand. "I was an American observer and Joseph was the caseworker dealing with a fourteen-year-old native girl who had been attacked by a pack of husky dogs that were running loose in the village," she shook her head in disgust. "It was awful, that child had to have a hundred and twenty-seven stitches to close the wounds in her face and arms. After the physical healing, her biggest challenge was coping with the emotional problems. Whenever she looked in a mirror she couldn't even recognize herself with all the scars on her face."

Joseph broke into the conversation saying: "Nick, I spent almost a week with the girl, and it was wonderful having so much good advice from Natalie. I knew then and there that I wanted to find a way for us to work together," he smiled, looking at the young lady he so obviously adored.

"I asked Joseph if he could use a little of his vacation time to come back to Alaska to help me on a case," Natalie squeezed Joseph's hand. "Of course, at the time, that was the best excuse I could come up with to see him again!" She smiled devilishly. "Nick, he was so naïve, he would have just let me walk away!"

A sheepish Joseph gave Nick a wide grin. "She set the trap — and I took the bait."

Natalie gave him a playful elbow in the ribs and said. "I mean, there really was a situation where he could be of help. We had a case where a young boy in Fort York had lost the toes on one foot from frostbite. He was not only having a hard time learning to walk again, but his parents had no idea how to cope with his temper tantrums and constant aggression. He seemed to be mad at the world. So, on his own time Joseph came as an unpaid observer — since then, we've been together!"

"I'm pleased, and very proud," Nick told them. "So, you are living and working in the Yukon now?" he asked Natalie.

"Ah, yes I am," she looked at him, strangely.

Red in the face, Nick mumbled something about that being good when it dawned on him they were living together.

For their outings with the children, Joseph and Natalie both used vans owned by the social services department. Joseph's was a nine-passenger, while Natalie's was equipped to carry twelve. There were eleven children going on the trip, both native and non-natives who came from desperately poor families. The eight boys and three girls, ranging in age from seven to sixteen years, had never been anywhere and had never before been camping.

Nick went with Natalie to pick up the boys while Joseph picked up the girls and all the supplies for their trip to the old mining town of Atlin in northern British Columbia. They met back at Joseph's place and set out in the two vehicles, Natalie driving in the lead.

Once in Atlin, they spent the better part of the day visiting the downtown area and later their group joined in with some local kids playing softball at the sports field. After the game, they piled back into the vans and headed south along the eastern shore of Atlin Lake. They set the tents up on a small plateau that provided a spectacular view across the lake and beyond to the magnificent Llewellyn Glacier. In the twilight, it took on an almost mystic quality, ideal for the telling of children's ghost stories.

When dark storm clouds moved in, they mounted a sheet of heavy plastic over the tents and an eating area in case it rained. Using the chainsaw Joseph brought, Nick cut five dead trees in eighteen-inch lengths and Joseph split them with an axe. Everyone pitched in and carried the wood back to where Natalie was preparing things for a campfire supper.

That night, sitting around the bonfire, Natalie asked Nick if he would tell the children one of his stories. From the broad smile on his face, it was plain to see that Nick loved telling stories. He asked everyone to move in a little closer.

"A long, long, time ago when the earth was still very young, a child was born into the Serpent River Indian band of Ojibwa. It was a boy child, and he was given the name Birchoggwin. Now, Birchoggwin had many attributes but the greatest one of all was a strong desire to help others. He was always helping someone in any way he could. He would help his mother at home or when she went out gathering firewood or picking berries. He would help his father cut trails through the bush, snare rabbits, or catch fish. He helped the elders gathering roots and herbs for making medicines. No job was so large, so small, or so difficult that Birchoggwin wouldn't pitch in and help."

"He doesn't sound like anyone I know," one of the teenage boys mumbled and everyone laughed.

"Ah, but wait," Nick looked at the teen and continued: "One day, a warring tribe from the south invaded the Ojibwa territory. Birchoggwin was the first young man to help defend their sacred lands from the invaders. He fought long and hard and when he paused in the middle of the battle to help a fallen warrior, he himself was killed. After the battle was over, Birchoggwin's body was brought home where he was wrapped in a pure white buckskin robe and buried on a hill overlooking the entire valley. His people missed him very much and wept openly for days after the funeral. In the spring when all the snow had melted and the flowers were starting to bloom, a strange and wonderful thing happened. From the exact spot where Birchoggwin had been buried, a young sapling emerged from the ground. It grew straight and tall, its bark as white as the new fallen snow and its branches covered with beautiful pale green leaves that reached for the sky."

The little seven-year-old girl sitting across from Nick stared in fascination, her eyes wide, her mouth open.

Nick paused, looking around at all the children. "The people had never seen such a beautiful tree before. One of the elders said that because it grew out of Birchoggwin's grave, it shall be called a birch tree. And the Creator, in His infinite wisdom, sent the wind to tell all the people about the magnificent birch tree and how it could help them in so many ways. The wind told them that in the time of the melting moon, its sap could be boiled and made into a sweet syrup that would rival that of the sugar maple. Its strong white bark could be peeled and made into food containers, baskets, and other fine works of art. They could also make watertight canoes that would carry them swiftly across lakes or down many rivers. Out of its strong inner wood could be carved smooth runners for their sleighs or tough frames for snowshoes and in the frigid moons of the winter season, it could be burned in their lodges to keep them warm and cozy."

One more time Nick paused, searching the eyes of each of the children. "That is why to this day, the mighty birch tree continues helping the people."

After finishing the story, Nick built up the campfire with wood and asked the children to each pull some grass and put it on the fire. When he told them that as soon as everyone was ready for bed he would set off some fireworks it brought a chorus of cheers.

Earlier that afternoon, a large bear had been spotted less than a half-mile north of the camp and Nick didn't want it coming any closer at night. He knew bears were afraid of grass fires and could smell them for miles. The fireworks he would let off for the children were actually bear-bangers, something designed to scare bears away. They would shoot up in the air about a hundred feet, then explode with a loud bang.

They spent the next day just east of Atlin fishing for Arctic grayling at Surprise Creek. Everyone caught fish except Joseph who happily spent all his time untangling the children's lines and cleaning their fish. The children each carried their fish back to their camp and when Nick prepared to fry them for supper, each child insisted they had to eat the exact fish they had caught.

That night Joseph, Natalie, and Nick sat around a flickering campfire and talked long after the boys and girls had all gone to bed. They had been quietly chatting for some time when the sound of a sniffle came from one of the tents. They stopped talking to listen and when the sniffles became more frequent, Joseph assumed one of the small boys was homesick and went into one of the boy's tent to check. When he opened the tent's flap and peered in, the little boy called Donald rolled over, trying to hide his tears. Joseph gently tapped the boy on the shoulder and in a whisper, asked if he wanted to get dressed and come with the adults for a talk.

The sleeping bag flew open and Joseph whispered for Donald to dress quietly and try not to wake the others. He waited outside with Natalie and Nick while the boy dressed. Then, as they walked around near the camp, Joseph asked the boy why he had been crying.

"I can't sleep."

"Are you homesick?" Joseph asked.

"Sort of. But I'm thinking about the boys in Whitehorse."

"What about the boys in Whitehorse?"

"They are always picking on me. They used to wait for me after school and once I was off the school grounds they'd beat me up. Now, if they see me anywhere, they start a fight. I don't ever want to go home again. I hate all those boys."

Then Joseph told him, "You know, when I was about your age I went through much the same thing. The boys in school used to beat me up, and when I fought back the teachers in school blamed me for starting the fights. I hated everyone, too."

"What did you do?"

"I did what a wise man once told me to do. He said, 'Do not hate your enemies, for if you do they will destroy you. Respect them, learn their weaknesses, and learn what makes them strong. Only then will you live in harmony with them. Do not hate anyone or anything. It will torment you, it will make you lonely, and you'll grow old before your time. Only love will give you peace and contentment. Love will lighten you heart and lighten your load as you go through life. It will bring you many friends and all your enemies will disappear'."

"Did all your enemies disappear?" Donald asked.

"Yes. It took a while, a lot of patience and understanding, but in the long run it was worth it. Sometimes it's easier to hate than to love, but if you hate less and love more, you'll become a better person. Now, do you think you'll be able to sleep?"

"I'll try," Donald sighed, yawning.

When they got back to Whitehorse Joseph went and had a talk with some of the boys that were fighting with Donald. Five of the six in the gang ended up going on their camping trip the following year. Donald eventually became good friends with them all.

CHAPTER 26

Joseph and Natalie's Wedding

A week before Joseph's wedding, Nick drove up from Vancouver, arriving in Whitehorse on a Friday afternoon. There was no answer when he knocked on the door at Joseph's apartment and no answer at Miranda and Dan's place, either. Only Leah was home and a delighted Nick got to spend time with her daughters. Chelsea and Brittany were a handful, and kept Leah busy. When Nick picked them up, they didn't stay long, too rambunctious to sit still for long.

Leah said that Tom was working somewhere around Steamboat Mountain on a highway project and Dan and Miranda were up at Inuvik but were expected home the next day. Joseph and Natalie would be back sometime during the weekend and would pick Nick up on Monday to take him with them to tour several remote Indian villages and meet some of the children they worked with.

Leah told Nick that Melissa was very busy at her new veterinary clinic. For the past few months there hadn't been a vet in Whitehorse so when she'd opened her doors, she had been swamped with customers.

"If you want, we can drop by and say hello. I'm sure she'd like to see you," Leah said.

"It would be nice to see her again. You know, I haven't seen Melissa since the Chilkoot Trail trip a few years ago."

When they arrived at the clinic Melissa was just coming out the door. Her face lit up at the sight of Nick and she scurried to greet him with a quick kiss. "I'm so sorry," Melissa said, "but I have to check on a sick elk at a ranch about twenty miles out of town. And I'm late already." She hesitated then her face lit up again. "Come on, you guys hop in with me and we can talk along the way."

At the ranch, after a short conversation with the owners, Melissa went straight to work. The sick elk, lying in the middle of a small pen, raised its head slightly when Melissa knelt beside it. She proceeded to take its temperature and at then ran her stethoscope over the elk's chest, at the same time asking the owner several questions.

Leah's girls watched through the fence as the elk calf, lying near its sick mother, stretched its nose and licked Melissa's ear and cheek. "The baby elk likes you, Melissa," Chelsea said.

"Males are all the same — elk or human," Melissa said looking up with a wink for Nick. She removed a needle from her bag, extracted something from a small bottle and injected it into the elk.

"Okay, that's all I can do for the mother right now." She told the ranch owner. Then turning to look at the calf, she said: "Now we'll see about getting some food into this little guy. Do you have a baby bottle with a nipple?"

The owner said he did and Melissa went with him to prepare a special milk formula.

When they returned, Melissa opened the gate and asked the twins to come sit on the bale of hay beside the fence. With the owner's help, she lifted the calf up and placed it across their laps. She gave Brittany the bottle and guided the little girl's hand to place the nipple in the calf's mouth. The calf latched onto it immediately and the twins giggled uproariously at the noises the hungry animal made.

While the children took care of the elk calf, Melissa walked over to Nick and said: "Now that I smell like an animal in the woods, you can give me a proper hug!" And she threw her arms around him.

Because Tom was away, Leah insisted Nick stay and keep her company for the weekend instead of going to Dan and Miranda's place. "The traveling is the only thing I don't like about his job," she told Nick.

They decided to pack up the twins and spend the day Saturday on the trails around Miles Canyon Park. Leah prepared a huge picnic basket with all kinds of goodies for them to eat. Sunday, they went downtown shopping and eventually ended up at a fast food place for lunch.

Joseph and Natalie arrived early Monday morning to get Nick.

They had the full week planned and wanted to make the most of it. Each day would be spent with a different group of boys and girls. Sometimes they would camp out overnight while other times they spent only a few hours together, playing games, making children's crafts, or going sightseeing.

The villages were spread across a vast area, meaning they had to spend a lot of their time traveling to their various destinations by van, by boat, and sometimes on an airplane or helicopter. After a week of traveling, they were back in Whitehorse on Friday night. A dedicated Joseph and Nathalie, filled with youthful vigor and dedication, worked at a hectic pace. It had proven a harder trip than an exhausted Nick expected and he knew then that this type of trip should probably be his last.

Joseph and Natalie had a small wedding planned for Saturday afternoon. Beyond family, they invited a few co-workers, a few friends from university, and of course, Jerry Beaumont.

The night before the wedding, Nick took Joseph out for dinner. The time had come for him to say what had been on his mind for some time.

"Joseph, the times we have had together each summer have been the best times of my life. Watching you and Leah grow up into good and decent young people has been the most rewarding thing I could ever have hope for. But, things have to change for you and me."

An uncertain Joseph said nothing, his eyes narrowing with intensity as he listened.

"I've never mentioned it before, it just wasn't important. But, a long time ago I was married — to a wonderful young lady. She had those same dazzling dark eyes as your Natalie." A distant, almost sad look covered Nick's face as he spoke. "The marriage didn't last and it took me a long time to realize it was totally my fault. I never understood her need to share time with me, or the loneliness I caused her. I worked long hours, and on weekends, too many of them, I went off with my buddies fishing, or hunting or camping or some other thing. I was young, Joseph, and I actually believed I deserved to relax with the guys because that's what men do. And when Christina — that was her name," Nick smiled at the sweet remembrance, "when she complained, I accused her of being selfish and trying to control me."

"Were your buddies all single?" Joseph wanted to know. "Coffee?" he suddenly added, looking over at the waiter.

"No, a cognac. Please." Nick said it with determination and a surprised Joseph ordered the drink.

"Yeah, one of them was still single, but two were married. Both divorced too, last time I heard. Anyway Joseph, the best thing that ever happened to me, up and left. I came home one day with a cooler full of trout but to an empty apartment. That was it, she was gone. It took me some time before I stopped blaming her, and for years I've had to live with the emptiness because of my own blind selfishness."

"Didn't you try to patch things up?"

"By the time I woke up, it was too late. She had married an architect from Toronto and the last I ever heard was from one of her girlfriends who told me she was happy and had three wonderful kids." Nick sipped the cognac, staring across at the only son he'd ever known. "Even out in the middle of the Yukon wilderness, not a night goes by when I put my head on the pillow that I don't think of her."

Nick stayed another week after the wedding and although he really didn't feel up to it, he traveled with Joseph and Natalie to her home in Katovik, Alaska. Unlike the last one, this tiring trip turned out much different than he had anticipated.

There were about a hundred and twenty people in Katovik, and most of them were related to Natalie in some way. For her family, they planned to have another wedding ceremony in the village, but one performed in the traditional customs of the Inuit people.

The night before the wedding, Joseph left some of his most prized possessions at the doorstep of Natalie's father. He left his rifle, a sheepskin, and the knife Nick had given him when he was a boy. In the morning the items were gone, which meant the acceptance of the marriage of his daughter to Joseph.

The wedding preparation lasted all day. It started out with the women of the village dressing Natalie in traditional Inuit garb. The men prepared Joseph, showing him what to wear and teaching him what to say to Natalie in the Inuit language on their first night. They laughed and joked with Joseph and even though he looked a little embarrassed, he was good-natured about it all.

Everyone from the village came to the celebration, from the very young, to the very old. One of the ladies, who claimed to be over a hundred years old, was doing an old Indian dance. There were many young children, some old enough to walk and some in papooses on their mothers' backs.

The feasting and dancing went on and on. First, the very elderly said good night; later on, the very young; then finally Joseph and Natalie slipped away. Now was the time for the young men of the village to display their skills and courage.

Dressed in their finest feathers and buckskins, all the bachelors gathered around a large bonfire doing their best to impress the young ladies. They all danced around the fire, then each man danced separately, spinning and kicking his feet as high as he could into the air. After each dancer finished, the ladies that approved would move in closer. If they moved back or turned away, it meant they weren't interested.

One of the older ladies yelled out, "How come Nick isn't in there dancing? He's a bachelor."

Some of the boys went over and carried him into the center of the ring. Nick feigned resistance for a while but when the drummers started beating their drums as loud as they could, he peeled off his shirt and started dancing, kicking his feet, tapping his toes and whirling as he circled the fire.

When he finished, all the ladies who had been quietly standing around the outside rushed in, pulling at his neck and arms and hollering, "I want him."

"No, he's mine," a very attractive widow hollered.

"He's coming with me," another teased.

The fun went on until well after the sun came up and somehow it seemed to help ease some of Nick's inner pain.

CHAPTER 27

Billy

FOR EACH of the next couple of summers, Nick spent at least a week touring northern communities with Joseph and Natalie. He would tell his old Indian legends over and over again. The kids never seemed to tire of them. He would teach the boys and girls the survival methods he had learned from the Indians, when he was young. He would also teach them how to identify the plants and berries that were edible, how to track animals, and how to tell the directions when in the bush, so as not to get lost.

On December 21st, four days before Christmas, Natalie gave birth to a nine-pound baby boy. When Joseph phoned Nick in Vancouver and told him, he flew up to Whitehorse the next day. It was only the second time Nick had been to the Yukon in the winter. The first being the winter they'd spent in the Nisling Valley.

Over the years he'd forgotten how cold it got, and how little sunlight there was in a day. The sun comes over the horizon for fewer than three hours before it sinks back down again. He had arrived on the shortest day of the year.

On the second day after giving birth, Natalie and baby Billy came home. It was wonderful spending Christmas with everyone. There was Dan and Miranda, Leah and Tom, and their daughters, Chelsea and Brittany, Joseph and Natalie, with son Billy, and of course, Dan's daughter, Melissa.

Nick stayed until January 4th, and before he left, he told Joseph that he wouldn't be coming back next summer. He was turning seventy years old and would be spending the summer doing a little golfing in Ontario.

Two summers later, they planed a two-day hiking trip on Mt. Cairnes, in Kluane National Park. Nick and Joseph were bringing young Billy along. They packed as lightly as they could. Joseph carried the tent, the food, and all the supplies, while Nick carried eighteen-month-old Billy, in his backpack.

Although Billy had never been away from his mother for more than a few hours since he was born, he knew something different was happening, and he was excited. Natalie had a tear in her eye when she kissed them all goodbye. She knew Nick and Joseph would take very good care of him, but she also knew she would miss him very much.

They drove up the Alaska Highway as far as Silver City, a deserted old mining town on the south end of Kluane Lake. They followed an old miner's trail along a dry creek bed that rose steadily out of the lush green valley below.

After hiking for less than an hour, they spotted a moose, standing in the middle of the trail ahead of them. As they approached, they could see it was a very old, skinny bull moose. Its coat was shaggy and matted. It stood with its head low to the ground and was facing away from them.

Wounded moose.

As they were making their way through the creek bed around the moose, it slowly turned its head and looked at them. As many times as they had witnessed death in the wilderness, it never seemed to get any easier. Half of its face was crushed in, its eyeball was hanging out, and there was blood coming from its mouth and nostrils.

They knew this to be the work of a grizzly and could do nothing about it. They carried no guns, only pepper spray for their own protection. They knew the grizzly would be close by, waiting for the moose to weaken before moving in for the final kill. They had to get out of there fast. Grizzlies don't like anyone hanging around their kill.

About eight miles up the trail was a flat, grassy knoll where they set up camp. Their global positioning system indicated they were at the fifty-six-hundred-foot level. It was over nine thousand feet to the summit and their camp was just over halfway up.

In the morning, they made their way around to the back of the mountain and to the base of the Kaskawulsh Glacier. From there they could see Mt. Logan, Canada's highest mountain. They spent the day sliding down the snow and ice at the base of the glacier and climbing the steep rocks above the tree line.

It was ten-thirty in the evening when they got back to base camp. The sun was still high above the horizon, and a warm breeze blew up the mountain from the south. There was lots of dry wood lying around, so they kept the fire burning twenty-four hours a day.

The next three days were spent exploring areas around the camp. The flats were covered with all types of wild alpine flowers. Although the lush green and purple heather dominated the area, fireweed, lupine, tiger lilies, and purple mountain saxifrage, were also in abundance.

On their way down the mountain, they came across bits of hair and bone on the trail. They knew it to be the remains of a once mighty and majestic animal.

The year after, Joseph, Billy, and Nick would be going alone again. They planned on canoeing up the east side of Lake Laberge and back down the west side. At fifteen miles long, it's the second largest lake in the Yukon. The high hills on either side and its shallow waters, make it prone to sudden rough waves. They would be travelling close to shore and were able to pull in, if the lake got too rough.

They used a sixteen-foot cedar-strip canoe that was fast but also very tipsy. Joseph paddled the stern; Nick was bowman; and Billy sat in a car seat in the middle. Any time it got a little too rough, they pulled into shore and hiked up the hills around the lake.

On the second night when they were camped at the north end of the lake, only a hundred yards from where it flowed into the Yukon River, they experienced something they would never forget or ever mention again.

It was just after dusk, the sky was overcast and thick fog had rolled in over the lake. Billy was sleeping on a blanket beside the fire, while Nick and Joseph were enjoying a cup of tea and some light conversation before turning in for the night.

Joseph was staring at a dim light that was moved slowly across the lake. After a while he asked Nick if he could see or hear anything out there. Nick turned and looked into the fog for a long while before saying to Joseph in almost a whisper, "I can see some kind of a light. It looks like it's on top of a smokestack of an old sternwheeler, moving towards the river. Only, no sternwheeler has plied these waters for the past fifty years."

"I can see what looks like a smokestack with smoke coming out of it, but I wanted to make sure you could see it, too. I didn't know if I was seeing things or not. If it is a boat, then how come there is no sound coming from the engine?"

They both watched in silence as the mysterious object moved towards the river and slowly disappeared into the fog. Without saying a word they crawled into their sleeping bags and went to sleep.

Over the years they never again talked about that night, or ever mentioned anything about seeing a sternwheeler steaming across Lake Laberge in the fog.

Shortly after returning to Vancouver, Nick quit real estate and moved back to Ontario, closer to family and his old friends.

That summer, Joseph and Natalie had committed themselves to working the villages along the west coast of Alaska and the Aleutian Islands. Nick flew up and spent two weeks with Billy and Leah's two girls, Brittany and Chelsea. He took them to the rodeo, to the circus, and swimming at the pool.

That was fine for the girls, but Billy wanted to go fishing or hiking in the mountains. He had all his gear packed and was ready to go at a moment's notice. Most were one-day trips, except for a two-day canoe trip they took from Watson Lake, up the Liard River. Billy loved the wilderness and the further into the bush they went, the happier he was.

He especially liked spending time with Nick, whom he called Gramps. Although he was only five years old, he would show Gramps all the plants in the bush that were edible, and tell him what their names were. He could identify any animal tracks, how old they were, and how fast the animal had been travelling. When Gramps asked Billy how he knew so much, he told him that his dad had taught him all about the bush and about the animals that lived there.

He said, "My dad is smart. He knows everything."

Nick only smiled and said, "Someday Billy, you'll know everything, too."

CHAPTER 28

Back to the Nisling Valley

TWO FOUR-WHEEL-DRIVE sports utility vehicles sat in the driveway with their back doors open. It was the first week in July, and Joseph was loading supplies for a five-day trip into the Nisling Valley. They were going to camp in the same spot where they had spent the winter more than twenty years earlier. Billy was running back and forth, bringing everything out for his dad to pack in the trucks.

Nick arrived in Whitehorse that afternoon, and the plan was to leave early the next morning. Everyone was anxious to make the trip this year, including Dan, Miranda, Leah, Tom, Brittany, Chelsea, Joseph, Natalie, Billy, and even Melissa, bringing her two Siberian huskies. They all wanted to visit the Nisling Valley one more time together.

Travelling the newly paved highway from Whitehorse to Carmacks was smooth and uneventful, but the road from Carmacks into camp was rough, full of deep washouts and large boulders that were sticking up everywhere. The trees had grown in on either side of the road, making it narrow and hard to follow. After only twenty minutes on the bush road, they had to stop and wait for a mother ptarmigan with her eleven chicks to cross the road in front of them.

The spot where they had always parked their vehicles was still recognizable. The small field where the horse had once grazed was now covered in lush green grasses and colourful wildflowers. As soon as they parked the trucks, Joseph arranged packs for every-one to carry, including Billy. The hike in was easy going, until they reached the river. The old riverbed had dried up and the swift-flowing current cut a new and deeper channel farther east.

Joseph tied one end of a long rope to a large tree, then waded across waist deep river and tied the other end to tree on the far shore. Dan hung on the rope and crossed with Brittany. Tom followed, with Chelsea on his back. Billy and Gramps were next, inching their way along the rope. Soon everyone was across. Melissa's two dogs were washed a hundred feet downstream, but were none the worse when they scrambled up the bank on the other side.

There was no sign of where the old camp once stood, and not a single fence post left standing. They couldn't find any part of the old corral or the sweat lodge, that over the years had fallen down and rotted away. No sign man had ever stepped foot in this land before. This small piece of land that was once slightly scarred had gone back to nature. Only the birds and animals were occupying it now, the descendants of the ones that had lived there before.

They set up the tents and built a fire pit on the sandbar along the river's edge. Leah, Tom, and the two girls had one tent. Miranda, Natalie, Billy, and Joseph the other, while Dan and Nick slept under the stars. The weather was warm and clear at night. The stars were so big and bright, made it feel like you could reach out and touch them.

The days were spent exploring the woods surrounding camp and at night they sang songs and reminisced around the fire. They even played some of the old games that had occupied their time so many years ago.

The salmon hadn't come upstream to spawn, yet there were plenty of Arctic grayling in the river to be caught. They would often see an old porcupine that hung around camp, and one morning they watched a cow moose with twin calves cross the river, downstream. There were a lot of tracks and droppings around from buffalo, but they never caught a glimpse of the herd.

On the forth day, they all headed for the Mountains. The weather was warm and sunny, with an odd black cloud hanging over the horizon. They brought rain gear along, expecting a sprinkle of rain throughout the day. As they made their way up the mountain, the showers turned into steady rain. They found a small cave, lit a fire, and all crowded in for lunch. As they huddled in a small cave, a bolt of lightning struck a tree not more than a hundred feet from the entrance, sending it crashing to the ground. All of a sudden the winds picked up, flinging branches and debris in every direction. The wind and thunder were deafening, as the rain poured down in sheets for almost an hour.

Soon, the sun came out and the skies cleared. Although the bush was still very wet and small streams of water ran down everywhere, the group continued along a narrow sheep trail up the mountain. When they reached a small, sunny, grass-covered plateau, they rested and dried their clothing before heading back down.

When they got back to where the camp had been, a flash flood had washed everything away; the tents and all their supplies were gone. There was three feet of water flowing over the sandbar. At that height, it was impossible to cross the river to go home.

First thing they did was build a shelter. As the axe had washed downriver, they used the knives they carried on their belts to cut branches, and pile them across a couple of poles tied to the trees. The waterproof matches they brought with them were in one of the backpacks that had washed away. Joseph and Nick, worked for two hours spinning a stick in dry leaves before they got a fire going.

Nick found a stand of bull rushes and picked and cleaned a large bunch of shoots. Joseph came back with wild garlic and some fiddlehead fern, he found on the south side of the hill. They used an old tea can he carried in his daypack to boil it in. That was their menu for the next three days, until the river dropped low enough to cross to go home.

CHAPTER 29

The Last Fishing Trip

O N A WARM sunny morning in the middle of August, seven year old Billy paced back and forth on the front porch of his house. He was waiting for Nick Roberts whom he called Gramps. Nick usually arrived there by the middle of June, or early July. This year, it would be later, because they were waiting for the king salmon run at Dalton Post, where they had fished together many times before.

"Da-a-ad; how long will it be before Gramps gets here?" Billy asked, in a long, sad, drawn-out tone.

"I was talking to him yesterday and he said that he'll be here on Friday," Joseph explained.

"How many more days until Friday?"

"Just five more days, that's all."

"Five more days, that long?"

Every summer, Billy could hardly wait for Gramps to take him fishing or hiking into the mountains. This year was no exception.

Billy had the tent and all the gear loaded into the truck days ahead of time. They would load the food just before picking up Nick at the airport. From there they would head straight out. The drive to Dalton Post would take them about four and a half hours and getting there early wasn't a bad idea.

Billy stood by the window in the airport watching plains landing and taking off. Every time an airplane landed he would ask, "Dad, is that Gramp's plain?"

"No; those airplanes are too small. Gramp's planeis a lot bigger." His dad would till him. Soon a large planelanded and taxied up to the terminal building. "We better go wait by the door. I think that might be Gramps now." Joseph said. They went down the escalator to the arrival door and watched as the passengers filed into the terminal building. They searched the crowd but Nick was no where to be seen.

Worried by Nick's absence, Nick, Joseph told Billy to stand by the door while he checked the passenger list. While waiting at the service desk, he noticed Billy jumping up and down. A minute later Nick came through the door, picked Billy up and swung him around. "Where's your dad? Did you come all by yourself?" Nick joked.

"No, he's coming right over there." Billy said pointing toward Joseph.

Joseph reached out for Nick's hand, hugged and padded him on the back. "Nick, how come it took you so long getting off the plain? We were worried about you."

"Oh it's nothing serious, I just dozed off a bit and they almost took me back to Vancouver with them. Anyway I'm here and ready to go fishing."

"I hope you're planning on a long stay, because everyone is expecting you to visit them. My mom is planning a big party when we get back from fishing."

"What's the occasion?"

"Because you're here, that's the occasion."

"Well if that's the only excuse for a party, I'm all for it. My return flight is in two weeks. That should give me enough time to see everyone"

"Billy will show you where the truck is parked and I'll grab your bags and meet you out there in a few minutes."

"Come-on Gramps," Billy said. "I've got everything loaded in and the truck. I even got your favorite fishing pole and reel. I bet we're gunna catch lots of fish."

They had barely reached the truck when Joseph came running across the parking lot carrying Nick's luggage. He loaded it in the back and soon they were on the highway, heading for Dolton Post.

When they reached the bridge over the Takhini River, Nick asked Joseph to stop the truck. Then they watched as he walked down the bank, dipped his hand in the water and rubbed it over the back of his neck. He stood there a while staring up and down the river. When he climbed back into the truck he motioned to go without saying a ward.

A few miles along the road he wanted to stop again. He crossed the ditch and slowly made his way up the hill. From there he could see the ranch house and in front, a herd of buffalo grazing in the field. His friend Cliff was gone and Virginia had moved on. The new owners were there now.

A mile farther down the road after pulling into Jerry's yard, they sat quietly in the truck staring at the cabin with all the windows boarded up and the empty coral overgrown with weeds. After a while Billy pipes up. "Who lives here?" he asked.

"A friend of ours, Jerry Beaumont used to live here. But he's no longer around," Nick explained." He hadn't heard from Jerry for years and wondered what might have happened to him. Joseph told him, the last he heard Jerry was living with his son somewhere around Carcross.

After leaving Jerry's place, they continued west on the Alaska Highway through the village of Champagne to Haines Junction. From there they drove south on highway #3 another forty miles then turned right along a bush road three miles, arriving at Dolton Post at three- thirty in the afternoon.

 Firstly, they set the tent up beside the river while Nick gathered wood, lit a fire and brewed a pot of tea. Joseph found an old dry log in the bush and set it beside the fire for Nick to sit on, then he and Billy went fishing along the river.

Nick sat by the fire sipping a cup of tea, as he watched Joseph and Billy make their way along the sandbar, tossing their lines with salmon roe attached into the river and letting them drift downstream. Half hour later Billy let out a holler. "Dad, I got one, I got one, and he's big. Help me bring him in."

"Keep your rod up. Don't let the tip touch the water. Let him run." Joseph told him as he grabbed the back of Billy's jacket to keep him from falling in the river. "Reel him in slowly. Keep the line tight." His dad coached, as they fought the fish up and down the sandbar.

Suddenly the line went slack. "I think you lost him." His dad said.

"What did I do wrong?" Billy asked with a sorry look.

"Nothing; when you have a tug-a war with a big fish, sometimes you win, and sometimes the fish wins." Joseph explained. Not long after Joseph had a fish on his line. He played it in the shallow water along the shore for ten minutes before Billy gave him a hand netting it. It weighed about twenty-five pounds and was more than enough for dinner. What they didn't eat, they cut into strips and hung over the fire to dry.

By six o'clock the next morning all their lines were in the water. Billy was first to hook onto salmon. "I got one, I got one," he hollered as he worked his way downstream along the sandbar. He tugged with all his might to lift the rod up, then he reeled in as fast as he could, lowering the rod at the same time. Then up again and reeling in, over and over, coaxing the big fish close and closer to shore. Joseph was there waiting and netted it in, before it had a chance to make another run and possibly get loose.

They cleaned it on the riverbank, and Joseph helped Billy carry it back to camp, where they hung it on a cross pole that they'd prepared earlier. It weighed in at thirty-two pounds and measured thirty-four inches in length. Billy was so proud of his catch; he wanted a picture taken with all of them standing beside it.

Soon after breakfast they were back on the river and by four o'clock, had their limit of six fish. They all worked to set up a makeshift smokehouse and by noon the next day, the fish were smoked, packed, and ready to be taken home.

The next three days they spent around camp, exploring the ruins of the old Northwest Mounted Police, post buildings. The Mounted Police had an outpost there from 1898 to 1905. From there they patrolled a vast area along the Tatshenshini River.

James Dalton established the first trading post at the site in 1894, where he traded supplies, with the Southern Tutchone people for their prized furs.

In 1898 when the gold seekers were passing through, heading for Dawson City, he charged a toll fee, often enforcing it at gunpoint. Due to the introduction of steamboats, and the White Pass Railway by 1902, Dalton sold his packhorses and deserted the post.

The morning they were leaving, Nick woke up early and had a big fire burning before Joseph and Billy were out of their sleeping bags. A heavy fog had blanket the aria overnight and the sun was just starting to burn its way through. Upstream Nick could make out the outline a grizzly-bear fishing with her cub. The constant sound of the water flowing over the rocks was occasionally droned out by flocks of low flying Canada geese squawking overhead, as they headed south for the winter.

Joseph poked his head out of the tent and asked, "Is breakfast ready yet?"

"No," Nick said, "but by the time you get washed up, coffee will be ready."

After breakfast they took down the tent and loaded all the gear in the truck. They had eaten one of fish they had caught the first day, and now were one short of their limit. They would try to catch a fresh fish to take home with them.

Billy fished right beside Gramps, while Joseph was trying his luck farther downstream. The sun heated the boulders along the river as the odd fluffy cloud moved across the light blue sky. The yellow, green and crimson leaves danced in the light breeze and sweet fresh smelling air filled their lungs.

It wasn't very long before Nick's line went tight; his reel screeched as the giant fish made a long run upstream, then all of s sudden the line went slack. Nick figured the fish escaped. As he reeled in about fifty feet, the line tightened again this time heading downstream. Nick held the rod up and pressed his thumb on the reel to slow it down.

Billy danced around with excited and hollered, "Gramps! You've got a big one! Don't let him get away! I'll go get the net from dad!"

Billy stumbled over the rocks along the bank down to where his dad was fishing.

"Dad!" he yelled. "Gramps caught a big one. Where's the net?"

"It's on the rock over there." Joseph told him, pointing to the net.

Billy grabbed the net and went running towards Gramps as fast as his little legs could carry him. Halfway back, he noticed a rod floating down the river. An immediate chill gripped his tiny frame. He sensed something very wrong. As he slowly approached, he saw his Gramp's body slumped over a large boulder. As he crept closer he called out in a loud whisper, Gramps, Gramps. When Gramps didn't answer, he ran back to get his dad.

Joseph knew in an instant by the horrified look on Billy's face, that something was serious wrong. He ran back along the bank with Billy, to where Gramps was lying. As he bent over and gently lifted Nick's hand, he realizes how bad the situation was. He immediately turned him on his back, pumped his chest with both hands and at the same time gave him mouth-to-mouth respiration. He worked on Nick for over an hour, hoping to find an ounce of life somewhere in that limp body. A body that had been a pillar of strength, for so many years for him and his family.

Then he turned and looked at Billy with tear-filled eyes, he said softly, "Billy, Gramps is gone. He's gone to visit the Great Spirit in the sky. I'm sure they can use a man like him in heaven."

Billy started crying uncontrollably. "Why did Gramps have to leave us now? We need him here more than anyone else."

His dad told him, "There comes a time when everyone and everything must pass on. We're only here for a very short time, and what we do with that time will be our only legacy."

ROBERT NICHOLAS KUCEY
Elliot Lake, Ontario

ROBERT KUCEY was born in the small town of Gypsumville in Northern Manitoba, Canada. As a young non-native boy he was very fortunate to spend a couple of winters living on the Dauphin River Indian Reservation with his family. His dad ran the general store buying fish from the Indians and selling them groceries, clothing, hardware and commercial fishing supplies.

He learned many things living amongst the Indians, things he would remember and use the rest of his life. He learned how they lived so in harmony with the environment. Every time they took something from nature they always managed to give something back. They didn't own the land; they felt they were part of it.

Although being dyslectic, and only completing grade eight in school, he worked at many different jobs and trades and ended up a top realtor in the Vancouver area. He is now living in Elliot Lake, Ontario, amongst many friends and family, working on his next book.

HANCOCK HOUSE *history titles*

Alaska Bound
Michael Dixon
ISBN 0-9639981-0-2
5.5 x 8.5 • sc • 190 pp.

Big Timber Big Men
Carol Lind
ISBN 0-88839-020-3
8.5 x 11 • hc • 153 pp.

Border Bank Bandits
Frank Anderson
ISBN 0-88839-255-9
5.5 x 8.5 • sc • 88 pp.

B.C.'s Own Railroad
Lorraine Harris
ISBN 0-88839-125-0
5.5 x 8.5 • sc • 64 pp.

Buckskins, Blades, and Biscuits
Allen Kent Johnston
ISBN 0-88839-363-6
5.5 x 8.5 • sc • 176 pp.

Buffalo People
Mildred Valley Thornton
ISBN 0-88839-479-9
5.5 x 8.5 • sc • 208 pp.

Captain McNeill and His Wife the Nishga Chief
Robin Percival Smith
ISBN 0-88839-472-1
5.5 x 8.5 • sc • 256 pp.

Crooked River Rats
Bernard McKay
ISBN 0-88839-451-9
5.5 x 8.5 • sc • 176 pp.

The Dowager Queen
William A. Hagelund
ISBN 0-88839-486-1
5.5 x 8.5 • sc • 168 pp.

Fraser Valley Story
Don Waite
ISBN 0-88839-203-6
5.5 x 8.5 • sc • 96 pp.

Gold Creeks & Ghost Towns (WA)
Bill Barlee
ISBN 0-88839-452-7
8.5 x 11 • sc • 224 pp.

Gold! Gold!
Joseph Petralia
ISBN 0-88839-118-8
5.5 x 8.5 • sc • 112 pp.

Great Western Train Robberies
Don DeNevi
ISBN 0-88839-287-7
5.5 x 8.5 • sc • 202 pp.

Harbour Burning
William A. Hagelund
ISBN 0-88839-488-8
5.5 x 8.5 • sc • 208 pp.

House of Suds
William A. Hagelund
ISBN 0-88839-526-4
5.5 x 8.5 • sc • 256 pp.

Jailbirds & Stool Pigeons
Norman Davis
ISBN 0-88839-431-4
5.5 x 8.5 • sc • 144 pp.

Mackenzie Yesterday & Beyond
Alfred Aquilina
ISBN 0-88839-083-1
5.5 x 8.5 • sc • 202 pp.

Mining in B.C.
Geoffrey Taylor
ISBN 0-919654-87-8
8.5 x 11 • sc • 195 pp.

New Exploration of the Canadian Arctic
Ronald E. Seavoy
ISBN 0-88839-522-1
5.5 x 8.5 • sc • 192 pp.

Potlatch People
Mildred Valley Thornton
ISBN 0-88839-491-8
5.5 x 8.5 • sc • 320 pp.

Quest for Empire
Kyra Wayne
ISBN 0-88839-191-9
5.5 x 8.5 • sc • 415 pp.

Walhachin
Joan Weir
ISBN 0-88839-982-0
5.5 x 8.5 • sc • 104 pp.

Warplanes to Alaska
Blake Smith
ISBN 0-88839-401-2
8.5 x 11 • hc • 256 pp.

Yukon Gold
James/Susan Preyde
ISBN 0-88839-362-8
5.5 x 8.5 • sc • 96 pp.

View all titles at www.hancockhouse.com